THE POINT

A NOVEL BY ANGEL I. HAWKINS

ISBN: 978-1-7343311-1-0 (Paperback)

ISBN: 978-1-7343311-2-7 (Hardcover)

ISBN: 978-1-7343311-0-3 (Ebook)

Library of Congress Control Number: 2019919236

Front cover image by Wilson Hawkins.

Book design by Angel and Wilson Hawkins.

Printed in the United States of America.

Originally printed in New York, New York.

www.hawkandquill.com

THE POINT

CONTENTS

Prologue.

You see, there's this girl. And not just any girl. This girl is THE girl. She is THE one. You know how we always search for THE one? The one that makes us that much better just because they are there to shed some sort of light in our life with just a look or a touch? The one that makes life worth living and makes you want to be the person that they deserve as well? Well I found her, but like every darn good thing that comes into my life, I lost her. I know, you're probably thinking, here's another story about a jerk who's going to proclaim that he's found the one and lost her doing something incredibly stupid.

But let me tell you how that's NOT the case. Yes, I've probably been a jerk at some point in my life, and yes, I found the love of my life, and yes, I may have done something incredibly stupid, but here's the kicker – it wasn't all MY fault. Bet you don't hear that every day. In fact, it was both of our faults, maybe even hers more so than mine but again that's not the point.

The point, dammit, is that I lost her and really want – no NEED – her back in my life. Maybe I'm crazy enough to think she would want me back or that I actually deserve her, but that's not the point either. The point of it all is not whether we deserve one another, because I mean, who can ever really know what one deserves? I can hardly make up my mind about what I want for lunch but yet I know that I deserve a woman as awesomely brilliant and perfectly flawed as Alice? No, it's not about deserving. It's needing and complementing and all that wonderful shit. Completing each other, you know?

I'll be honest, I don't get mushy about much, but when I lose something I really care about, I get mushy. I'm human, hell. Am I not allowed to get mushy and sentimental and crap? But right, the point. The absolute point of why I'm telling you all this is real and complex and deep and won-derful and scary and stupid and crazy and just IS all at the same time. The point I am getting at is when you find some-one who you absolutely cannot live without, who really and totally completes YOU – and I'm not talking the artificial you that you create in your head to please everyone, but the real God-honest YOU – the one hardly anyone, if anyone at all, knows – the inner turmoil and twisted, dark you that even you weren't sure fully existed YOU. If you found this person who gets that and I mean really gets THAT, then for God's sake, you fight for that person and win back that per-son and do whatever it takes to get that person back in your life forever. How do you do that? you may ask. Well that's the point…

The Point

Summer.

Okay, so this one day, this hot summer day must have been in like August, you know? Because most hot days happen in August. I guess hot days exist in July, too, but if you want truly hot days, you don't feel 'em until August. But that's not the point. The point is it was a hot August day, and my buddy Rich and I were just hanging in his backyard. Typical white suburban neighborhood where everyone has manicured lawns and curvy driveways and two-storied houses and backyards and shit. That kind of neighborhood.

Anyway, my buddy Rich and I were just sitting on lawn chairs in his backyard next to his pool. You see, in this neighborhood, you either have a pool or a trampoline, or both. Rich just has the pool; I have both. We were just chilling, you know. We sort of have this rock band and all of our equipment is in Rich's bathhouse, which is why we were hanging there. Mike and Bill had left after our session to help cook dinner or set tables for dinner or some dutiful son stuff like that. So here Rich and I were. You see, Rich is probably the closest friend I have, the brother I never had but always wanted.

So we were just talking and all of a sudden I said, "Rich, you know what I really want?"

Rich rolled his eyes as he flipped through his guitar magazine – he's always rolling his eyes or flipping through a magazine because he's used to my crap by now. "Sure, what is it, Willoughs?"

Here's another thing. I have the weirdest name ever, so everyone calls me by my last name. My parents thought it was cute to name me after some long dead relative, but I honestly prefer my last name than to be called that shit. And you better not ask me what my real name is or I promise I will sock your eyes out.

"I want a black girl," I retorted.

Rich scoffed and turned the page in his magazine yet again. "What prompted this, dare I ask?"

"What do you mean, what prompted this? Aren't you bored living here? Don't you want something new? Dude, we're starting college in a month and we've always been stuck HERE. It's time for a change!" I replied.

"All right, why don't we try the new Mexican place downtown like I've been telling you guys? Casa Rosa or something like that," Rich said.

"No, I mean let's really do something dude," I pleaded. "We should totally drive to that barcade in Richmont and pick up chicks and shit."

"Do you hear yourself, man? College is coming soon enough, you can get yourself killed there," Rich replied.

"See, that's what I'm saying, Rich. We make all these crap songs about adventures and love and stupid things but we never actually do them!" I argued.

"Willoughs, how about this? My sister's friend Rebecca is having a party this weekend over at Greenpoint. Since you want to have this out-of-body experience so badly, we can go there, scope out the college chicks, drink, smoke, whatever. You'll get a piece of the college experience before actually entering college. And I know some Mexicans that live in that area, so there's your diversity quotient all in one!" Rich proclaimed.

You see, one thing about Rich is that every time I get an idea, he always already has the solution up his sleeve.

Why couldn't he mention this before he mentioned that dumb Mexican restaurant crap, I don't know. Who eats at a restaurant for excitement, right? Or maybe he saved this suggestion for last because he knows I hate parties. The whole situation is awkward, you know?

And by parties, I mean house parties. Like it was somewhat cool in the 90s but kids nowadays don't know what a good party is. Everyone just stands around drinking from red cups, grinds, or go full throttle and fucks. The next day you hear of people who drank too much and vomited, police arriving to break any would-be fun, or if you stick around long enough, you hear Christine got pregnant. No one really goes to enjoy themselves anymore.

I'll tell you the best party I've been to, perhaps even the only party I've ever been to, other than those birthday parties thrown by my parents – you know the ones, with five-year-old kids with water balloons and punch and too much cake – yeah those. But anyhow, the best party I've ever been to was thrown by Lutherans. Now they know how to party.

You see, my mom made friends with this new girl's mom who moved into the neighborhood, Lucy was her name, and her family. Well Lucy's family was Lutheran and had started to make friends at the local church, and Lucy's mom wanted her to have more friends and whatnot, so they decided to throw a party so Lucy could get more acclimated to the neighborhood. They invited all the Lutheran church kids, Ivan the weird kid down the block, and me. Of course I didn't want to go because I hate parties, but of course my mother accepted the invitation for me and there I was.

See, Lucy wasn't that bad looking. She could actually be described as cute. She had short brown hair and all these cute little freckles around her nose. Sue me for thinking freckles are cute. But the thing about Lucy was that she was so terribly shy and awkward, that even saying hi to her seemed to give her a heart attack. However, when her folks finally left us bunch of kids alone in the basement is when everyone started having fun. The Lutheran kids actually played good music —current music — and danced! And I mean really danced, not the stupid grinding and twerking dances that people seem so fond of these days. Like they actually incorporated aerobics and shit in their moves. They faced their partners and you actually had to have moves in the dancing.

I had so much fun dancing and learning how to dance that the lack of alcohol and Lucy's awkwardness didn't even matter. We even played Pin the Tail on the Donkey and it was a blast. Now you know a party has to be good if someone gets excited playing that game. But I digress.

Sure, Rich had a great idea with the party and even though part of me didn't want to go, it just felt like something I should do. So of course, how did I reply to him?

"Let's do it, man, I'm totally down. You know I love parties!"

Rich smirked to himself and continued flipping through his magazine.

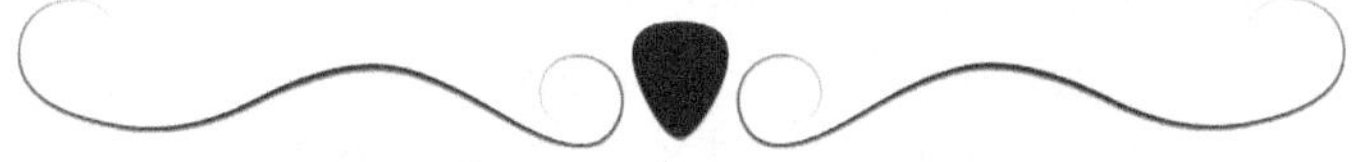

See, I knew this was a bad idea. I felt it right before Rich and I left. But did he listen to me? No.

"C'mon, Willoughs, stop being a pussy and man up! You're the one who wanted to go out!" Rich pleaded.

So here I am, standing in the corner by myself as usual. Rich took one girl upstairs and God knows how long they're going to be. Rich's sister, Jan, left early with her jerk of a boyfriend. Rebecca, the girl who hosted this stupid party, is chucking up her dignity in the backyard. Great. Some party.

Then the worst of it happened. I was standing there considering joining the stoner kids for a hit when this girl fell onto me, spilling my drink all over the both of us. "Watch where you're going, jerk!" she exclaimed.

"Excuse me? You fell onto me!" I grunted under her.

This girl didn't seem to know how to get up, and every time she attempted, she fell closer and harder onto my stomach, which made me want to rethink that quesadilla from earlier.

"Maybe, maybe I wouldn't have fallen onto you if you l-looked where you were g-going!" she stated.

Just my luck, another drunk. "Okay, off you go." I shoved her off my stomach, which tripped up this other guy.

"Dude, what's your problem? Nobody knows personal space anymore. You see, back in my day…" he started until Jerry from the debate team escorted him away. Drunks, right?

I looked over to the girl now that I had a better view of her, but the poor thing was totally gone. She snuggled up into a fetal position on the floor with this interesting smile on her face. I pushed her mass of raven curls from her face and noticed her eyes were closed. I could've just left her there. I probably should have but the way she just seemed so vulnerable got to me. I mean if my little sister was balled up onto the floor at some party like that, I would want someone to be nice to her too and make sure she was alright.

I tried to pick her up, but to no avail as we both ended up crashing onto the floor again. For the life of me, I don't know why I couldn't pick her up; she wasn't some huge girl or anything and she was actually pretty tiny all things considered. However, sure enough, this rustling finally woke her up.

"Honestly? I told you to watch where you're going!" she exclaimed and then she clocked me. This tiny girl clocked me hard! I mean I literally saw stars. I clutched my nose as blood seeped through my fingers. Thankfully, Rich came down right around the same time I'm sure my broken nose laid in my hands.

"Willoughs buddy, are you okay? Hold your head down, man. Who did this to you? Sit down, man," he proclaimed worriedly.

One thing I can say about Rich is that he always shows up on time. Not necessarily when you want him to, but when he's supposed to be there. His girl Trish or whatever ran to get me an ice pack, but the sight of the blood nauseated me all of a sudden and I puked just a bit into my hands.

"Relax man, you're good," Rich reassured me and patted my back as my head went reeling.

I looked up at that moment and saw the curly-headed girl. She had these huge brown doe eyes and looked at me with a mixture of confusion and worry. Her sort of mocha skin almost seemed flushed from what I thought to be sympathy. Interesting.

Before I could muster the energy to ask her name or even nudge Rich as to the culprit of my broken nose, she gave a penitent look and scampered away. Or maybe it seemed like she scampered away, because how could she really do that when she couldn't stand up by herself a few minutes ago? But then my head started reeling again and I passed out.

Crap. I didn't even get her name.

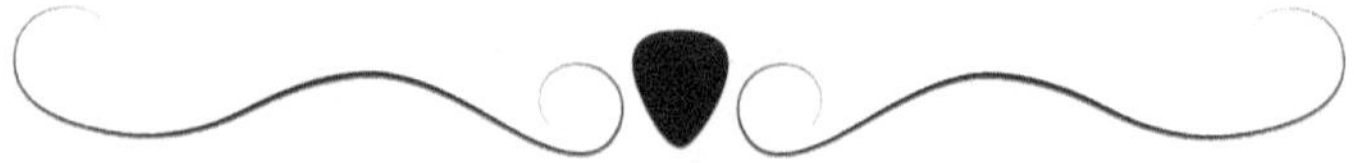

Sure enough, I wasn't imagining it. My nose is broken and now I have to wear this stupid patch on my face. My face got red and purple around that area, too, and trust me, that is not a flattering color on me. I'm already a redhead and we get enough rap as it is.

"Hey man, it really could be worse," Rich tried to comfort me.

I guess it could have been worse, but I just grew into my face. Girls were starting to think I was cute and all, and now this broken nose is going to take me back to that awkward phase all over again. Maybe I can explain that I was defending the honor of a damsel in distress, or maybe say the other guy got out of it worse than I did and got two black eyes. That would be awesome.

"Willoughs, what did you do now?" my mother demanded.

You would expect her to run to my aid or fix me some soup or something, but alas, she too is used to my crap. I swear I can't wait for college to start.

"Nothing, mom. It was something stupid. I fell and bumped my nose onto Rich's kitchen counter," I mumbled.

"Tsk, tsk. I guess it would make sense. My baby is growing so fast that your legs just can't keep up with your face," my mother responded.

Yeah, that's another thing. I've gotten super tall the past year or two, and thankfully I was finally able to shed the baby fat. Shit was cramping my style.

"Yes, I reckon so mother." I ran my hand through my disheveled hair.

"Well you go rest up, Willoughs. Rich, thank you for letting him sleep over at your house, and apologize to your mother about his accident for me. Oh! And tell her I tried that green bean casserole recipe and still can't make it as well as hers! What does she put in it? You know what, I'll give her a call myself – it's been ages!" my mother declared.

"Sure thing, Mrs. Willoughs, and yeah I'll definitely apologize to her again about Willoughs' accident." Rich smirked in my direction.

"Yeah, get out of here, man. Tell Bill I need my pick back for practice. We're still on for tomorrow, right?" I clapped him on the back.

"No doubt, man, rest easy," Rick clapped back and left.

"Willoughs, what am I ever going to do with you?" my mother chuckled as she shook her head and went back to peeling the potatoes. She already had water boiling and meat loaf on the side, spiced and ready for the oven. I observed her as she did this and noticed that she looked tired. Her blonde highlights were surely returning to their mousy brown color and her blue eye shadow seemed a bit much today as she had icy blue eyes already.

"Do you need help with anything, mom?" I asked sincerely.

"I'm fine, Willoughs. You tend to yourself. I'm sure you must be tired. I'll call you down when the food is ready," she smiled wanly. I kissed her on the cheek and ran upstairs to my room.

When I entered my room, I saw that my little sister Ella had left a picture for me on my bed. Little siblings are the greatest. I lifted it and half-smiled at the scrawled lettering, 'To the bestest big brover, Willoohs'. Cute. She gave me flaming red hair and purple eyes. My eyes have the tendency to change colors, I've been told, but are usually a greenish-blue. Although I can see why she gave me purple eyes, my eyes are blue around her because she makes me so happy. She's a good kid.

"Will-oohs?" I could hear her voice behind me. I turned to her with the biggest smile.

"Will-oohs! Your face is purple like the picture!" Her light blue eyes widened. She resembles mom, since they both have those icy blue eyes and same mousy brown hair. Dad has sort of dirty blonde hair and eyes that resemble mine. My red hair is the only oddball in this family. Well, among other things, like my compulsivity and natural anxiety-ridden tendencies.

"Yeah Ella-Bella, I had a little accident and now my face is purple. But I'm okay, I promise," I tried to reassure her.

"No! Fairy Berry can help you!" she pouted. Great, my sister is cute and all, but once she gets started on the Fairy Berry shtick, it takes a while to calm her down. She goes into this whole routine of pulling out her wand and twirls and sings this song and stuff, but it gets oh-so-tiring after a while.

"Yes, I know Fairy Berry can help, Ella-Bella, but right now I'm really, really tired. How's this? I'll take a little nap and when I wake up, Fairy Berry is the first person I'll call to heal me. Okay? But it won't work if I'm really tired, okay?" I bend down to her level so she understands me and press her hands.

She looks at me for a minute with doubt, finally lifting

from her brow. "Fine," she relented.

"Thank you so much, Ella-Bella. Give Willoughs a kiss!" I push my face close to hers.

"EWWW!! I don't want no purple on me!" she shrieks and runs out the room. Unfortunately, she's learning about cooties all too fast in that preschool of hers. About a year ago she would've snotted on me to make me feel better. Oh well, her loss.

Finally, I'm able to lie down in my bed. The most comfortable bed to ever exist on the planet, the heaven-on-Earth type of bed that if you let yourself close one eye lid on this mushy, plump water bed, you'll never want to leave type of bed. Yes, this is the bed Maroon 5 sung about. No homo.

And then I drift off into bliss.

"One, two – one, two, THREE, FOUR!!" shouted Mike, as he clicked his drumsticks into rhythm. His dark wavy hair flips back and forth as he gets into his psyche. Bill and I wait our turn to start adding in the guitar, while Rich stands center stage, eyes closed, waiting for cue.

Soon, electricity sparks from our fingers into the guitars, and I stamp on my amp to get the pitch just right. Bill's fingers go crazy over the strings and we nod to each other, yes, we're finally in sync. I glance over to Rich who pulls the mic to his mouth and sings, "Your sweet surrenderrr evades me/I don't know how I can resist/You give me something tender/ So moist, so twisteddd…" Yes, he's working his magic. His raspy voice registers well through the room and I feel then that we hit our stride.

I look over to Mike, still in tune, still feeling the percussion in his bones. Bill and I are set, but as always in these bands, Rich is the true star. The one girls fawn over and daydream about. I mean, sure, he has the good looks that typically follow the lead — chestnut hair, hazel eyes, tattoos, and the right muscle tone girls gush about. I can't fault him for that. Heck, he even has the talent. His voice is wicked nice and has almost an old-soul feeling to its raspiness that's just right for our sound. But this is just practice and he sounds amazing. As he should, since we're performing tonight at our favorite spot, Sal's. Sal's is this pizzeria downtown that almost everyone who's anyone in Fernwood has been to. Sal has known us since we were born, and we've opened here from time to time, but tonight's the first time we have the entire night to ourselves.

"...Why not? You boys will be leaving me and going to college, about to embark on the best times of your life. You should have one more good memory before you leave," Sal said in his throaty Italian accent when we asked if we could play here. I swear I saw the big guy wipe away a tear. "Damn onions always get to me." Sure, but I'll miss this place, too.

It has some good memories. I remember I brought Lucy here a couple times, you know, after she got over her awkwardness. "Willoughs, it smells like sweat and feet in here," she scrunched her freckled nose. Yeah, it did but it was our sweat-and-feet pizzeria that always served those anchovies just right and soda too loose. Man, the nostalgia gets to me. I heard State had some authentic pizzerias, though; the boys and I should definitely check it out.

"Your sweet surderrrr…" Rich trails off his last note. Da-da-da-tisss, Mike strikes the last beats of the drums, and Bill and I break from our guitars.

"Alright guys, I think that last set was pretty sweet!"

Mike nodded excitedly. He wiped the sweat from under his huge tussle of dark hair. I shake my head in agreement and notice we're all drenched in sweat. Something about Sal's brings that out, I guess.

"Yeah, I think it was a good run. Yo, it's freaking hot in here. Rich, come grab a smoke with me outside," Bill sighed. He yanked his guitar over his head, and pulled at his shirt to air himself. His pimply face shone extra bright today and I could tell he was overthinking about tonight.

"Cool cool, man. Look, we did great, we're ready. You'll be fine tonight, man," Rich slapped his shoulder.

"I guess. Right now, I'm not even thinking of that. I'm burning and Sal always has that heater on!" Bill reasoned. It's true. Sal seemed to be going through man menopause lately.

"I feel you," Rich agreed. "Hey guys, let's break for now, eat and whatever. Show is in three hours so we can definitely squeeze in one more practice in a bit. I think we should do "Antacid" when we get back, say, in like a half hour?"

"Bet," we all agreed.

As Rich and Bill left, I hung back with Mike and grabbed water from Sal's fridge in the back. Plopping myself in the wooden chair close to the stage, I surveyed the pizzeria trying to etch every crevice in my mind. The hardwood floors, long mahogany countertops, Sal's homemade style pies on display, and that lovely sweat-and-feet smell. I definitely need an anchovy slice before I leave this place.

"We'll come back to visit at least once or twice a month, Willoughs. I'm going to miss it, too," Mike read my mind.

I tilted my head up to him, gave a half smile, and said, "I guess so." But we both knew that those who left Fernwood hardly ever came back.

Right in the middle of our set is when the curly-headed girl came again. It's funny how a tiny thing like that girl could just make an entrance. But she wasn't alone. She came with some great burly guy who looked like he belonged with an ax and some log cabin in the most obscure bumb-a-fuck. Although obviously I didn't care but seriously, how could she handle a guy like that? Or how could he handle her without breaking the poor thing?

She flashed her straight pearly white teeth and seemed to glow as he led her to a high top table for two. Her raven curls bounced with every step she took and her skin looked so warm and inviting, like honey. When she finally looked up to the stage, her smile faltered slightly at the sight of me, but quickly magnified in its brilliance. This girl was smiling from ear to ear like nothing happened.

I looked over to Rich who was nearing his last notes and then on to our crowd. Most of the crowd was smiling and cheering appreciatively, but these were people we all knew growing up. Mrs. Baker, the florist down the block, and Dr. Smith, the dentist practically everyone went to. Yet somehow when she came in, I started to feel more self-conscious. I looked to Bill, who didn't miss a note or twinge at all, and Mike was drumming his heart out. And soon enough the set was finished, and the crowd gave us a standing ovation.

Rich breathed into the mic and said, "Thank you everyone for coming out tonight. We all appreciate your support over the years and we're so happy to perform for you all before we move onto our next step. We're going to have a little intermission, if you will, and perform some more for you guys in a bit. We'll catch you in twenty!"

The crowd started murmuring to themselves and shuffling and screaming loudly. Rich faced us and started, "Okay guys, we're doing good—"

"Rich!" I hissed at him.

"What? What's your problem?" he asked, taken aback. "That girl, the one who did this to my face, is right there," I pointed in her direction.

"Where? Where is she?" Soon all the guys were clamoring on top of us to scan the room.

"You guys make it so obvious, fuck," I muttered. "It's the black girl with the curly hair, sitting next to that fat guy. Right there next to the entrance."

"Huh, she's pretty cute, Willoughs. I'd let her punch my eyes out." Mike ran his fingers through his dark hair.

"Not bad, Willoughs, but how'd you let that pixie beat the shit out of you?" Rich commented. The other guys snickered.

"Yeah, haha, very funny," I shrugged.

"Poor Willoughs, you let her deck you and she's going out with a guy uglier than you!" Bill tried ruffling my hair.

"Okay, can you guys cut it out? She's not that cute, and besides I don't think drunken brawls exactly count as a fair fight," I tried to reason. Sometimes I wonder how I made friends with these buffoons.

"Yeah yeah, Willoughs, whatever. Although I don't know if it's just me but she looks very familiar, and I can't put my finger on where I know her from," Bill furrowed his brow.

"Dude, how would you know her? I know everyone you know," Rich reasoned.

"Yo, I swear I know her from somewhere. I don't know or remember how but I've definitely seen her before," Bill stated. He started rubbing his stubbly chin as if he was contemplating algebra.

"Well in any case, don't let her get into your head, Willoughs. We have like four more songs left and I really want "Antacid" to go well, alright? I thought I heard you slipping near the end of the last song," Rich became serious. One thing about Rich is that he is so intuitive and notices everything when it comes to his music.

"I'm not, relax." I was starting to get annoyed. Rich raised his brow, giving me that look that meant he really means business.

"Alright, break guys. C'mon Bill, let's go for a smoke." Rich beckoned Bill. Bill glanced a bemused look at me and patted me on the shoulder on his way out.

"Those guys." I shake my head and look for Mike. Mike smirked and ran his hand through his floppy black hair, using the other hand to take a swig of a bottle of water. I moved over to the amp and sunk down, wiping sweat off my face as well.

"Man I will definitely miss this place, Willoughs," Mike began. "It's home here. I know we're not going to be too far from here, but there's nothing like home. This place is just full of memories…you think we'll be okay out there, in college?"

I look over to Mike. He hasn't had the best of luck in life. His dad skipped out on his mom and he had to work two jobs all through middle and high school to help out at home. One thing about Mike, though, is that it always seemed like he had a vendetta to be better than his dad. The town knew all about the story and sent sympathy pies; I remember my mom was one of the many to help out. Although quite honestly, Mike is one of the smartest guys I know and the fact that his pops would do that astonished me. I knew Mike was going to make it, though; he always did.

"Definitely, what are you saying? What's with all the Debbie downers tonight? I thought tonight was supposed to be fun and happy," I stated. "You and Bill need to lighten up. This new chapter we're about to start is for the better, trust me when I say that, Mike. We'll come back often to perform and you're always going to be great. You will make an excellent accountant, so don't worry too much. It all works out in the end." I felt almost as though the last bit was more for me than Mike.

Mike, seemingly assuaged, grinned and placed his hand on my shoulder. "Thanks Willoughs, you're right. I just needed a sounding board, but you know what? It will be alright! And since you're so confident about our future, how about you go make moves on that cutie over there? Maybe she isn't with that guy, because she keeps looking over here…"

My ears perked up. I look slyly over in her direction and surely enough, she was eyeing me. I braved a longer look and stared right into her big doe eyes. She blinked once. Twice. Then she broke into a huge smile, bit her lip, and gestured for me to come over to her. At that instant, I felt my legs go numb as if I were paralyzed. I noticed the crowd murmuring. Sal was making a call in the kitchen behind the counter, Rich and Bill were laughing at something excessively funny over their cigarettes, the lumberjack was walking to the men's room, and I felt a clap on my back.

"Dude, she wants in! You better go over there and make a

move or I'll swoop in and get her myself. She's really cute, what you waiting for?" Mike enthused in my ear. Yet somehow my body just wouldn't move. I turned back to her direction and much to my chagrin, she stood right at the foot of the stage.

"Hey, I think I saw you the other day at the party, right?" this curly-headed pixie asked. As if she didn't remember, ha. Maybe she didn't, she did seem to have drank a few that night. Wait, why can't I speak?

"Well hello there, I'm Mike Nichols and yes, you did meet this strapping young gentleman the other night. I'm only sorry I couldn't have met your acquaintance as I had other matters that evening," Mike replied for me, in the most annoying British accent ever. He crouched forward and took her hand. "And, fair creature, what is your name?" I could feel my insides churning at this gross attempt at flattery. Perfect timing to act weird.

She glanced at me, amused, before turning to him and attempting a pretty spot-on British accent. "My name, kind sir, is Alice Atkins. I'm afraid I have been misfortuned as well to not have the pleasure of meeting you. Although I don't think I was quite in the right spirit, if you may, to give an honest impression, as I'm sure this lad has dispelled onto you." Mike raised his eyebrows in delight before kissing her hand. "My my, witty as well as charming! Forgive my friend, he gets quite star struck in the presence of beautiful women."

Kill me now, please, just kill me.

Alice giggled politely, which seemed to finally break the ice. "I'm sorry, I was having a long night. I'm Willoughs," I finally mustered. I could feel my cheeks redden. Great, another joy of being a redhead.

Alice looked to my nose and almost sheepishly remembered the impression she left upon my face. "Oh my gosh, oh my gosh! I am so sorry for doing that to you!" She reached up to my cheek, which made it worse, almost inflaming the damage more.

"Oh this? Please, you hardly left a scratch! I'm just wearing this so that my fans won't be thrown off by a little scar," I brushed off. Mike stifled a laugh as he could call my BS. Even Alice could call my bluff. Darn, I thought I was good at hiding it. Maybe I should rethink my poker face.

"Well in any case, I apologize again and wanted to tell you guys that you sounded great. I was going to wait until after the show but seeing as I recognized you, I thought I'd come and say something now," she said matter-of-factly. "I think your sound is really cool. I hardly visit here but my brother wanted to come out and check the local scene."

Brother?

"Brother? That guy was your brother you came in with?" Mike mirrored my exact thought.

"Yes, my big brother, Mason. Why? Did you think that was my boyfriend?" Alice replied slyly.

"No-" I started.

"Heck yeah!" Mike interrupted. "If you don't mind my asking and I'm not too rude but--?"

"Why? I can't possibly have a brother who looked like that because I look like this?" Alice snapped. She raised an eyebrow and crossed her arms over her chest.

"I'm sorry, that's probably ignorant. What I mean is…" Mike started again.

"Haha relax, I always get the stiffs with that one," Alice pushed Mike's shoulder. "I was adopted and that's my big bro." She flashed another smile and both of our shoulders eased with this reassurance.

Suddenly, I heard footsteps coming up the stage behind us and Rich asked, "Okay guys, are you ready to start in like two minutes?" Rich and Bill came up behind us, and Rich, like the Casanova he is, caught eye of Alice. "I'm sorry, am I interrupting? My name is Rich by the way, lead singer of this group, Left Red Door." He squatted down to extend his hand. "And this is Bill here on the second guitar," Rich gestured to Bill, but he was twiddling with his guitar and threw up a complimentary wave.

"Nice to meet you all, I'm Alice," Alice greeted, shaking his hand. "I was just telling these two how great your band sounded and to apologize to this guy for the other night." She smiled and looked over to me, causing me to turn away.

"That's right! I was just wondering how Willoughs could let a tiny thing like you beat him up, but I see why," Rich winked. Oh God, any minute now he's going to pull the classic one liner and she's going to fall for him like they all do.

"Yeah, well, I've been known to throw a couple good punches. I have a black belt after all, fair warning for you not to get on my bad side," Alice winked back.

"Rich, we have to start soon!" Bill shouted from behind, sounding anxious.

"Right, I'll let you guys get back to your gig. Hey, do you guys want to stop over at my place after? I have a free crib and some people coming over anyway, it'll be cool," Alice started backing up, but kept her eye on me.

"Yeah, sure, definitely," Rich and Mike said. Pathetic, right? These two losers. I shook my head to myself. Alice noticed me, laughed to herself, then somewhat shamefaced, reiterated, "All of you guys. Willoughs, you're coming too, right?" Mildly surprised she remembered me, I stammered, "Yeah-yes! I'll be there!"

Beaming, she replied, "Awesome! By the way, nice name." She walked back to her table, hands in her jean pockets, curls bouncing with each step.

"Willoughs man, good job," Rich grinned in my ear as he went to straighten his microphone. I shrugged my shoulders as Mike gave me a look of approval.

"Whatever man." I could feel my face burning as the other guys gave me looks of approval.

Rich gave a single shoulder shrug and said, "Suit yourself," then turned to the audience and starting to growl in his signature raspy tone. "Are you guys ready for MORE??!!"

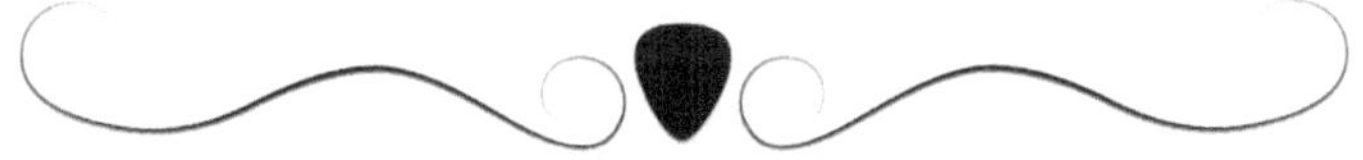

So Alice neglected to tell us a pretty significant detail. Sure, she wasn't lying that she was adopted, or that the lumberjack Mason was her older brother, or even that her last name, which should've been a red flag to us sooner, was Atkins. In fact, that should've given us a bigger clue than anything else she sputtered to us.

As we drove up behind her and her brother and saw the mansion that waited for us, that's when Bill came to his senses. "What's this girl's name again?"

"Alice, Alice Atkins, I think she said," Mike replied.

"Shit! That's how I know her!" Bill hit Rich on his shoulder.

"Crap Bill, what do you mean that's how you know her? And careful man, I'm driving!" Rich said, annoyed.

"She's Councilman Atkins' daughter! He's the one who signed for the increased tax on cigarettes, alcohol, and soda! They had a write-up on it in the paper and a picture of the family. I knew I had seen her somewhere!" Bill exclaimed.

"You're serious? Her dad's the reason why half of my paycheck has to go to my smokes now? I almost liked her," Rich shook his head, grinning at me. "Willoughs, maybe if you get in good with her, her dad can repeal that decision."

"Haha, Rich. They should tax the heck out of those cigarettes, you're killing yourself, dude," I replied.

"Yo, no wonder it looks like she's loaded. Willoughs, I didn't know you had it in you to bag someone like this!" Mike shook my shoulders. "Would you look at this place? It's beautiful!"

We all gazed at the entrance as we pulled up to it. Mason reached out to punch in a code for the gate to open for us to enter. The driveway was curved into a semi-circle around a fountain that stood in its center. The hedges were all manicured perfectly, some into shapes of cupids, on the sides of the entrance. Multi-colored begonias were circled with stones, and there was even a mini pond on the right side of house. There was one long black limo sitting in front of the house, and a cherry red Benz behind it.

The house itself was spectacular, made of stone with columns holding one balcony over the mahogany door. Many windows of what I supposed were like ten bedrooms faced us and it appeared that there was someone home as the living room light was on, and a gold and diamond chandelier shone brilliantly on the left of the front door.

Mason and Alice pulled up behind the Benz as we followed suit, parking behind them. Alice hopped out of the car, tugging at her leather jacket, and beckoned for us to follow.

"Willoughs, before we go in, let me just say this. If you find yourself slipping at any point, give me a signal and I'll take over, okay?" Rich said seriously.

"Would you relax? I've seen better houses than this. My aunt, you know the one who lives in Virginia, has a house that's at least three times as nice as this," I started.

Rich rolled his eyes. "Willoughs, I've met your aunt in Virginia and trust me, it's nothing compared to this. Besides, we're not here visiting your aunt, this is different."

"Okay...while you guys are sitting here discussing the merits of visiting relatives, I think I'll go in and say hi to Chives," Mike stated. Sure enough, there was an older man holding a tray with what could be presumed to be hors d'oeuvres. I wouldn't be surprised if his name tag did read Chives.

"Yeah, let's go. If Willoughs does mess this up, at least we'll get a good story out of it," Bill reasoned. If only they gave me more credit.

Alice tapped on the front window, asking, "What's taking so long?" and giggled. Meanwhile, Mason stood next to his car looking as if there were a million other things he would rather do than babysit high schoolers, like down about five trays of biscuits. On that note, we clamored out of our minivan, which seemed to pale so much in comparison to her house, almost as if we were there to clean her pool.

"You guys are funny, come on in! Edgar has some shrimp puffs here. Hopefully none of you are allergic or else we could get you guys something else," Alice said as she walked towards her house.

As we followed her, I could feel the cool breeze emanating from the fountain, a very welcome reprieve for the humid evening and clustered van. Mason shuffled ahead of us into the house, hands in his pockets as a middle-aged woman opened the door. When we went up the stairs and into the foyer, we could hear music reverberating off the walls lightly. Stepping into the lobby, all that surrounded us were golden floors and mirrors on the sides of the door. Edgar took our jackets as we gazed up to the ceiling, which held up works the likes of Renoir and Van Gogh.

"Cecilia, I thought my parents were out for the evening," Alice wondered to the middle-aged woman.

"They were, but they brought home guests a little over an hour ago, dear," Cecilia replied, taking Alice's jacket.

"Hmm. Well then, can you look for some towels and trunks for my guests? We'll just hang out in the bath house. Edgar, show these guys there and take whatever they order for snacks. I'm going to change, if that's fine with you guys?" Alice inquired us.

"Sure, sounds great," Rich replied for us.

"Gentlemen, if you would follow me," Edgar curtly addressed us. Rich and I exchanged looks of bemusement as Mike gaped open-mouthed while we followed Edgar. Bill looked incredulously around him and Mason shook his head at all of our reactions before he moved on with Cecilia elsewhere.

We walked to the left of the entrance and through the dining room, which held the majestic chandelier, through the kitchen with its marble-top counters and three ovens. And past the service people's quarters where several maids and cooks were conversing or ironing or playing cards. We went through a long hallway past a large laundry room and a couple of guest bedrooms until we finally reached the bath house. As if the house wasn't impressive enough, the bath house made us all catch our breaths.

Harp music was playing and bounced off the pool waters. The Jacuzzi was bubbling away and several angels observed us as we made our way to the poolside chairs. The floor had golden marble so shiny that we could see our reflection clearly through them. The room had a glow about it, perhaps from the floors and mirrors. There were plants on the sides of the bath house that comprised of lilies and hydrangeas.

Edgar droned in a bored manner and asked, "Would you gentlemen care for some appetizers and drinks as Cecilia gathers your pool trousers?" We glanced at each other. How much is really too much, you dare ask?

"Can we have some caviar?" Mike asked.

"Meat supreme pizza and beer for me," Rich quipped.

"Sushi?" asked Bill.

"I'll have a Coke and fries," I offered.

"Very well then, gentlemen," Edgar bowed and regally walked away. When we could hear his footsteps finally subside in the hallway, we all snickered to ourselves full force.

"Can you believe this? I could get used to someone waiting on me hand and foot!" Mike fell onto the padded beach chair.

"If only. We have to make it, guys," Bill replied as he started taking off his shoes.

"Willoughs, have I ever thanked you for being the best brother I never had?" Rich laughed.

"Yeah, this is pretty sweet!" I agreed.

Cecilia entered with four pairs of swimming trunks and huge beige towels in tow under her arm. "Gentlemen," she smiled politely. We each grabbed one, and feeling the trunks' material, I could literally feel the richness coming off onto me. Silk slipped my fingers and the tough elastic waistband fit perfectly on my hips.

Rich and Mike did cannonballs into the pool while Bill sat on the edge waving his feet in the water. I decided the Jacuzzi would be more my speed and walked over when Alice, Mason, and a tan girl walked in.

Alice wore a white bikini with gold accents that complimented her brown skin greatly. She managed to pull her curls up into a neat bun with a couple ringlets caressing her cheeks. Mason had on red trunks similar to the ones I myself had chosen, and the tan girl had on a pink and purple striped bikini and a long blonde ponytail.

"Hey guys, this is my best friend, Chelsea. We're roomies in college and have been close since forever," Alice waved her introduction. "That's Bill here, Rich and Mike in the pool, and Willoughs over there in the Jacuzzi."

"Hello, Chelsea!" the guys all said in unison.

Instantly, I saw a shift in attention from Chelsea to Rich. Yes, I thought. That's more his type anyway.

"Hey guys," Chelsea said, acting aloof. She whispered something into Alice's ear, which caused her to smile a little. Mason moved on over to the opposite side of the pool and dipped his feet in. Alice and Chelsea set their towels onto two pool chairs side by side and headed in my direction.

"How are you liking the Jacuzzi? Did you try the massage option?" Alice asked lightly.

I looked to the sidebar of the Jacuzzi and noticed the option for that. "I guess I wasn't really paying attention," I said sheepishly.

"That's like the most basic function. How could you miss that?" Chelsea rolled her eyes.

"Chelsea!" Alice hissed.

"What?" Chelsea seemed bewildered. "It's an honest question and a pretty obvious one, too. Hey, where are you from, William?"

"It's Willoughs and I'm from Fernwood," I replied matter-of-factly.

"Hmm, that's about two hours from here, right? Decent town as far as towns go, I suppose. So how do you know Alice?" Chelsea asked.

"Well I…" I started.

"Chelsea, can you go see Edgar about what you'd like to eat? And see how long it'll take for it to get here?" Alice chimed in and eyed Chelsea down.

Chelsea looked from me to Alice, raised her shoulders and said, "Fine, whatever. I was just trying to make conversation." Chelsea rose from the Jacuzzi, grabbed her towel, and walked out with Rich and Mike's eyes fawning over her.

"Excuse my friend, she can be a handful sometimes but she means well," Alice said.

"It's fine. I'm used to being interrogated," I responded.

Alice laughed lightly and asked, "So do you go to University as well? I'm assuming since you were at Rebecca's party."

"Well, I will be starting next week," I said, feeling a little embarrassed. Of course she would be older.

"Nice, freshman. I remember those days like they were yesterday," she smiled. "I'm going to be a sophomore this fall. You're going to love it, though, and with your band, you're going to be a hit. You should definitely play on campus sometime." Not too bad, only a year difference.

"Yeah, actually the boys and I were wondering if there's a place like Sal's nearby where we can perform. We'd like to be more local and get our name out there," I said.

"There's Freddie's, which everyone goes to and should be no problem. And there's a coffee shop I work in called Sips that has a homey feel," she replied.

"Great! We have lots of songs and have been performing for about six years now, but definitely want more profit from it. I mean, I'm going in as a physics major, but music is a passion of mine," I stated. "What are you interested in?"

"That's cool. Physics seems a ways off from music but I can see music being steady. I'm actually an English major, aspiring lawyer, and advocate," Alice said proudly.

"Really? I'm guessing your dad had an influence on that decision? But wait, shouldn't you major in government and politics or something?" I asked.

"Well as an English major, you're taught to analyze texts and read between the lines to understand what the author or writer is trying to convey. I think it'll be very useful in studying law and contracts my clients will inevitably get themselves into. And besides, I love reading and writing, so naturally it would be a perfect fit," Alice asserted.

"Well it's cool that you have it all figured out. I usually find that people who major in English are smart people who don't know what to major in," I said.

I had read it in an interesting article that offered that sentiment since people always seem to dog English majors. Hey, physics isn't the most appealing major either, but Mr. Zutelli taught it well enough in high school that I thought, why not give it a try in college? I'm not the brightest bulb in the box, but when I get something, I really get it. School has never been one of my strongest suits but something about physics resonated with me, and no way would my folks let me major in something like music.

At that time, Edgar wheeled in a cart with our entrees and drinks, as Chelsea hung by his side sipping at what looked like a glass of champagne. How fitting.

"Wow. You know, you could actually find those in every major," Alice retorted.

Quickly realizing my mistake, I started, "No, I know that. I'm just saying that oftentimes an English degree isn't that useful in the real world and so then these otherwise smart people are left to squander for some mediocre job that doesn't use them for the talents they're trained with."

"Excuse me?" Alice questioned.

Uh oh. I glanced over to Rich, who was chatting up Chelsea as he drank his beer. Edgar came over with a tray of fries and my Coke. The fries seemed to be every variation a fry could be: waffle, salted, peppered, sweet potato—like fry heaven. I grabbed a handful and shoved it in my mouth to prevent from answering.

"You're a piece of work, Willoughs. Let me show you something," Alice huffed. She took hold of my hand, yanked me from the Jacuzzi, and wrapped a towel around herself.

As we passed Chelsea and Rich, two different sets of looks embraced us. Rich's eyes widened in approval and encouragement, the bastard, while Chelsea's eyes widened as far as her Botox could allow, almost in disgust. She even muttered, "Ew," and turned back to Rich, slapping his stomach to silence his approval.

I looked to where this pixie was leading me when I noticed she had a tattoo on the lower side of her back of three swallows circling each other. Interesting.

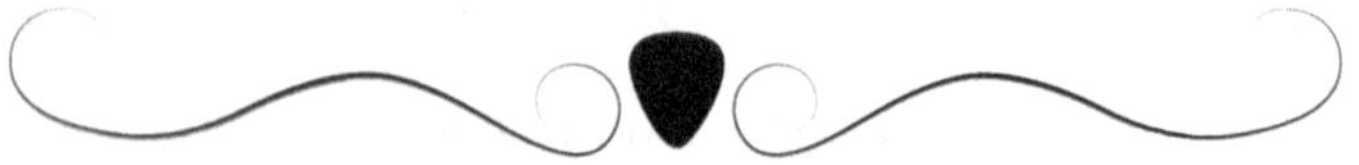

She led me to her bedroom, or auditorium as I could imagine it. I instantly smelled rosewood and lavender. Her walls were painted a turquoise color, but the posters that hung were peculiar. She had black and white photos of Malcolm X and Martin Luther King, Jr., James Baldwin, Maya Angelou, Erykah Badu, all with their respective quotes. Yet there were also posters of Nirvana and the Rolling Stones.

Her bed was huge and had linen similar to the walls. When I walked in, I saw a vanity mirror on top of her cream-colored chestnut chest of drawers with several girly items like hairspray, scrunchies, gel, makeup, a jewelry box with a twirling ballerina, several pictures of her family members, and a stool. Heck, she even had a piano in her room. Yet on all of her posters, she had post-its filled with more quotes and sayings.

I peered at the sayings as she went to her attached bathroom, I'm guessing to freshen up. One post-it read: "To Thine Own Self, Be True."

Another read: "When I was five years old, my mother always told me that happiness was the key to life. When I went to school, they asked me what I wanted to be when I grew up. I wrote down 'happy'. They told me I didn't understand the assignment, and I told them they didn't understand life. – John Lennon"

Both of these were placed at the top of her mirror.

Looking further, I saw two pictures that I thought were intriguing to place near each other. One picture showed a younger Alice with pigtails and dimples, probably about six years old. Mason stood next to her with a crew cut, a more slender frame, and a sort of mischievous smile on his face. Councilman Atkins stood behind them with Mrs. Atkins, both probably in their mid-thirties and beaming. Mrs. Atkins was sporting a blonde mullet-looking hairdo that seemed to be all the rage in the late 80s through 90s, while Mr. Atkins had a thick brown mustache, glasses, and a brown suit.

They all looked so happy, and Alice looked as though she belonged there. The picture next to the family shot was of a woman who looked like Alice would look in about ten to fifteen years. She was highly attractive with the same smile as Alice and deep dimples. Her hair was straightened in the picture, falling well below her shoulders, with honey blonde streaks that became her brown complexion. Though her smile seemed beaming, her eyes seemed sad somehow, as if she knew something tragic would happen. It seemed obvious that this woman was Alice's birth mother.

"Okay, Willoughs, since you think English majors have no use in society, I'll have you know that Supreme Court Justice Clarence Thomas was an English major, Steven Spielberg, our governor, and the list goes on," Alice showed me in this report. I noticed she had put jeans on and a flowy cream top that showed off her body well.

"I understand completely, and I'm sorry for—whoa, Sting and Vin Diesel were both English majors?" I snatched the printout from her hand.

"Yep, you can find us in any facet of life," Alice crossed her arms, giving me a one-sided smile. I browsed the list of people as Alice plopped onto her chaise in front of her mirror. A white spunky shih tzu suddenly scurried into the room onto her feet yipping for attention. "Jackson buddy, I've missed you all day!" she snuggled into the fur ball.

I smirked at the sight of them. It almost seemed reminiscent of the spirit of her younger self. "If you don't mind my asking, how'd you come to be adopted by the Atkins'?" I asked curiously.

"That's a bit personal for one night," Alice chuckled softly. "But apparently my mother and the Atkins' were good friends in college. So when my mother passed away, they took me in since I had no other family. My mother had me with some bozo from college who wasn't of any help, so they tell me, and they just adopted me as their own. I was about four when they took me in." Alice's face turned serious.

"I'm sorry to hear that. Sorry for pressing you," I suddenly felt uncomfortable. Death is always a touchy subject and I've never been good at dealing with the topic.

"It's fine. Things happen. I'm just fortunate that the Atkins' took me in and loved me like a family should," Alice shrugged.

"Did your biological dad ever come into the picture? Like at all?" I wondered, something about that detail struck me.

"Nope, although it is something I've wondered about. I mean, how could a supposed attractive, smart woman fall for someone who didn't care enough to look after their child? But in all honesty, who cares? I have a family and that's what matters," Alice shrugged.

"Yeah, that's all that matters, I guess," I said. I couldn't even begin to imagine what it would be like to be adopted and have a piece of your identity out there somewhere, living and not caring about you. The thought spooked me. I blinked at Alice, who appeared amused at my pondering of this.

"You're funny, Willoughs. Let's get back down to your fries."

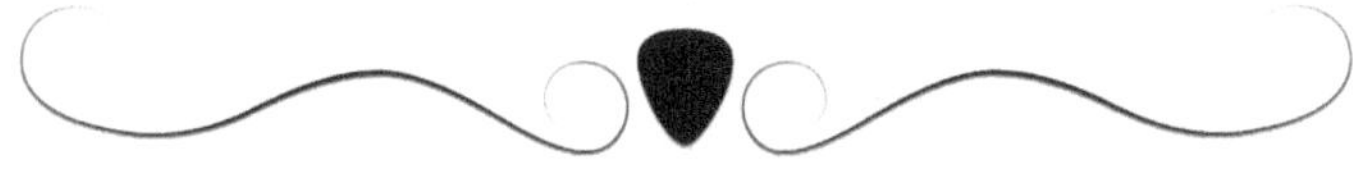

This is why I can't bring my parents anywhere. They're so freaking embarrassing, it's not even funny.

"Willoughs, honey, put on your University hoodie and let's take a picture near the sign," my mother chirped. Rich laughed at my discomfort. "Rich, you too, you know your mom would want a shot of your first day moving in!"

I mouthed "hah!" to Rich, who threw a paper ball at me. Thankfully, we got to be roomies, with Mike and Bill sharing a room down the hall. Our stuff was unpacked as best as possible and our room faced the main building where our classes would be held. Ridgewood State University. I pulled the red and grey hoodie over my head despite the heat. The bulldog insignia of our mascot growled out under the University name. I guess one thing I could be proud of is that we have a good football team.

"Will-oohs go grrr!!" Ella mimicked the school's namesake.

"No, Dad goes grrrr!!!" my dad bellowed as he picked up Ella. Ella shrieked in delight as he tickled her.

"Evan, please be careful with Ella! Oh, what am I going to do with you all?" my mother shook her head, though she too had to work to keep the smile off her face. They had Ella so long after me, after so many failed attempts to get pregnant again, that my mom took extra caution with our little roughhousing.

"Aww Gracie, we're just having some fun," Dad reassured her. He placed Ella down and pecked my mother on the cheek.

"Okay, I'm ready to take the picture!" Rich said, mock posing in his University sweatshirt.

"Alright then, let's get on out there," mom said as she pushed us to the door. She turned to me and said, "Willoughs, if you need anything at all, you let us know, okay? We're only a phone call away. Now when you're here, you're going to have to be responsible." She wagged her finger at me at the last order.

Dad, walking not too far behind, reiterated. "Willoughs, you listen to your mother. Mind your drinking and partying, we're paying too much money for you to screw it all up. Get involved, find a job, and build your resume." They both looked at me sternly. Honestly, it's like I never get credit around here. You would think that years of working at Sal's and putting my energy into the band would prove responsibility. Heck, I graduated in the top fifty of my class. Shouldn't that count for something?

"All right, all right, geez! Get off my back, I'll be fine. I'll make you proud." I held up my hands defensively. They exchanged slightly worried looks before descending down the stairs.

"Don't worry, Mr. and Mrs. Willoughs, I'll keep an eye on 'em!" Rich came to my rescue.

"I think that worries me even more," dad rubbed his eyebrows.

"Evan, be nice!" my mother elbowed him. "Rich is perfectly aware of how special Willoughs could be!"

Honestly, I'm right here. Rich lifted Ella up onto his hip as we exited the building and draped his other arm over my shoulder. "Yeah Mr. Willoughs, you don't have anything to worry about!" Rich cheesed up to my father, who only shook his head and clapped Rich's back.

"I suppose so."

At that moment, a Frisbee landed in front of mom, causing her to shriek in surprise.

"Sorry about that!" Bill cupped his hands from across the lawn. He and Mike had already settled in, leaving me to wonder when my folks would get the hint. He squinted over at us while Mike ran over to pick the disc.

"Oh, never mind me, I'm just getting older and ready to flop," my mother clutched her chest. "Now you two come over here. Willoughs and Rich are about to take a picture!"

"Sure thing, Mrs. Willoughs," they agreed. They sauntered over to the sign cut from stone and metal bearing our University name. I loped on over, wrapping my arm around Rich and Mike's shoulders as Bill took up the other end, left of Rich. Ella had wriggled her way from between Rich and Bill, and squatted down to smile for the picture in front of my legs.

"You boys look so handsome, college men!" my mother exclaimed cheerfully. She dug into her purse for her digital camera as my father stood beside her, hands on his waist. His hair had some grey on the sides above his ears, and when he smiled, crow's feet gathered near his eyes. I looked beyond them as my mother rummaged for the camera and onto the lawn where coeds were pulling boxes, refrigerators, and pillows from their cars on pulley carts and taking them to their respective red brick dorms. Some people, having already unloaded, were laying out on the lawn on blankets, propped up on their elbows or wearing shades and sunbathing.

A couple were tossing a Frisbee a few yards away. I squinted from the dorm building we had just left in time to notice a certain brown-haired, freckled girl I hadn't expected to see.

"Smile guys," my mother managed to pull her camera in time to snap us before Lucy could say, "Willoughs?"

Now see, I thought Lucy and I ended on good terms. I went to her party, which turned out to be a lot of fun. I did the nice thing and took her out to Sal's a couple times. I respected her enough to tell her the truth all the time, even when I broke up with her. Quite honestly, it wasn't me, it was definitely her. You know how those breakups go. Oh, I swear it wasn't you, it's really me. I have to work on myself.

Yeah right. I already have my own problems without having to worry about hers as well. Poor girl had so many issues. It wasn't just the awkwardness, but her family was so messed up. Her mother eventually left her father for her secretary, her dad lost his job and went into a depression, and Lucy here gained a few pounds and slit her wrists. It was literally too much. I told her so. Although really, if she lost the weight, I would've considered staying. Which I also told her. So much for honesty.

But in my defense, this was two years ago. People forgive and forget all the time, right? Not Lucy. She kept this façade that we were still together for at least a year after we broke up, stalking our band's rehearsals and gigs and butting in when a girl thought to look my way. After a while, she just disappeared. Rumor had it that she and her dad packed up to live with family in Alaska. Another rumor had it that Lucy was put into a mental hospital.

Apparently all those rumors were untrue, as Lucy stomped over in our direction just as mom finished taking her pictures. She stood not too far from my dad, arms crossed with a half-smile on her face. She let her hair grow longer and it was nearly touching her butt. She seemed more tan with some freckles sprinkled on her nose and shoulders. She definitely lost the weight and appeared taller and more toned. She was wearing a red halter top with white shorts and green flip flops. Well her sense of style might be questionable, but overall she looked healthier, and more like her former self.

Rich pinched my shoulder as my mom snapped the last picture, causing me to hiss and yell, "I know!"

My dad turned around to look at where the voice was coming from and saw Lucy. "Lucy Wilcox, how are you? We haven't seen you in a while!"

"I know, right? It has been a while," Lucy acknowledged before my dad gave her a bear hug.

"Lucy? My God, you have grown into a pretty young lady! Why it must have been two or three years since you last stopped by!" my mother exclaimed, finally done with pictures.

"Loose-y, loose-y!" Ella jumped up and down before running over to dad's side.

"Great, can this day get any better?" I muttered to the boys.

"I guess it could, Willoughs boy," Mike ruffled my hair.

"Wait, I thought she moved. And why is she here? I would've thought she'd attend Yale or something," Bill wondered.

It was true. Before the family scandal, Lucy was one of the brightest of our class. She would've been accepted to any Ivy League given her grades and extracurriculars.

"Obviously not," Rich stated. "Willoughs, you should play nice since it looks like we'll be seeing her a lot more often."

I bit the inside of my cheek as I watched my family have a mini-reunion with Lucy. My parents had liked Lucy well enough. Or even more so. My mother was delighted when she found out we were dating and would bring up Lucy long after we broke up. My dad thought she would be a good influence on me, and though Ella was merely a toddler when we were dating, she had a fondness for her as well.

"Lucy, you must stop by for dinner from time to time," my mother announced, hands on Lucy's shoulders. Please, God, no.

"I'd love to, Mrs. Willoughs, but I don't think Willoughs would care for that too much." Lucy smiled in my direction.

"Nonsense, you simply must try my roast. I've gotten a lot better at preparing it over the years, mind you. Besides, Willoughs wouldn't mind, would you, Willoughs?" she passively asked before returning to Lucy. "Oh and we must catch up! You know I've always thought you and Willoughs made the cutest couple! Just the other day I was remembering your first kiss. You remember, right? And Willoughs turned so red…"

"Mom!" I shouted, feeling my own face as I remembered

the event.

It was hella awkward like everything else. After our second date at the movies, Lucy's parents dropped me off at home. Lucy walked me to my doorstep to wish me a good night while her parents coasted down the street to idle, trying to give us some privacy. I was a little nervous but knew I had to get it out of the way before I wound up a kissing virgin for the rest of my life. I leaned in and planted a wet one on her nose by accident. She scrunched her face and laughed, which made me realize my mistake, before she grabbed the sides of my face and moved it to her mouth.

At this point, I had braces, but it didn't seem to matter that I partially scraped her inner lip. I was finally kissing Lucy Wilcox! Although I couldn't help but feel as though someone was watching us, and sure enough, there was my mother peeking through the glass next to the door taking pictures! When she realized I saw her, she tried to discreetly run away, only to knock into my father who was coming down the stairs. Talk about embarrassing.

"Oh yes, I remember, Mrs. Willoughs," I could sense Lucy was amused and slightly embarrassed at the memory. "But if you'll excuse me, I really have to go. I just thought I'd stop to say hi." Lucy started to back away from my parents, glancing nervously at me.

"Right. Please don't let us keep you! Tell your father I said hi and do stop by from time to time. Know you're always welcome," my mother replied.

"I'll keep that in mind." Lucy placed her hands in her front pockets. "I'll see you around, Willoughs" Lucy said as she skipped away to the opposite side of the lawn.

"Willoughs, I never thought I'd say it, but after these last couple of weeks, I think I want to be you when I grow up,"

Mike stated.

45

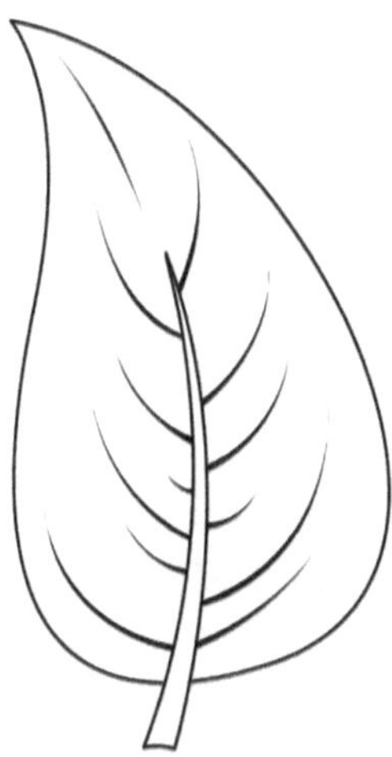

Fall.

"**W**illoughs, you think you could stock the shelves in the back," Amanda thrusted a box full of sweatshirts at me. She looked extra Goth today as her black eye makeup was exaggerated, and her long black nails nearly cut me in the process of handing me the box.

"Sure boss," I uttered tiredly. I had to pull an extra shift at the college bookstore since Ross was out sick even though I really needed to study, rehearse some chords, and sleep. Most importantly, I needed sleep. Or coffee at the very least.

A gangly guy with wide gauges stepped into the store and asked, "You mind if I place a couple flyers in here?"

"Go for it," I replied. I lifted the box to carry to the back of the store. The guy threw flyers up around the sales floor, sticking them where he could before sauntering over to me.

"Hey, I'm Thomas and the local colleges are throwing a talent show, trying to find the best of the best around. Grand prize is $40,000, second is $10,000 and down from there. It's sort of a tradition we have here." He offered a flyer to me. His arm had several prominent tattoos. "Maybe you know of some local talent? The auditions are in a couple of weeks and the contest itself will be held in the spring."

"Thanks man, I think I know of a group." I took the flyer.

"Sweet!" he grinned. "Thanks. We're hoping to make this year a good one. Take care!" He waved on his way back out of the store.

Amanda emerged from the worker's room adjusting her jacket and skirt. Jared, her boyfriend, came up behind her, grabbing a cigarette from behind her ear.

"Willoughs, clean up these flyers before you lock up for the night. I think I'll have to implement a new rule of no more outside advertising." She shook her head.

"Sure boss," I expressed in the same tired monotone.

Jan walked in and said, "Amanda, Jared, are you guys ready?"

"Yeah, give us a minute, your kid brother's friend just let someone put up papers all over the place. I swear you can't get good help anywhere nowadays," Amanda replied, agitated.

"Willoughs!" Jan exasperated. Jared sniggered off into the corner.

"Hey hey, relax. I'll clean it up. You all just go out and have fun. Let me slave away for my paycheck in peace," I replied.

Jan rolled her eyes. "He's right, let's go, Amanda. I don't know why you get so worked up over him."

Amanda gave me a dirty look before relenting. Jared ran his hand through her hair and down her back to ease the tension. "Fine. Lock up the registers and stockroom before you leave, okay? We close at one a.m. today. Tony should be here in a few to take over for Elliot flipping burgers, but I want you to make sure everything closes up."

"Gotcha," I nodded.

In the two months I've worked here, only once did I forget to lock the supply room. You'd think she'd let up. Only a stack of pens were missing. As if this place couldn't afford to lose $51.48.

"I'm serious, Willoughs," Amanda warned. I went back to stocking the shelves with the sweatshirts and replied, "Noted."

When she determined all was well, she grabbed a hold of Jared's hand, with Jan stomping behind them.

I decided to play Nirvana's "Smells Like Teen Spirit" to lighten up the place. I swear that song always makes me feel better. I don't know what it is about it.

As the song picked up, I snatched a broom from the supply closet and swept to the song, fully rocking out. Never mind that I had a ten page paper due at the end of the week and hadn't started. Never mind that I hadn't completed the lab for my intro physics course. Never mind that midterms started next week and I hadn't studied as of yet. Never mind any of that when Kurt Cobain yelled the insecurities of the generation.

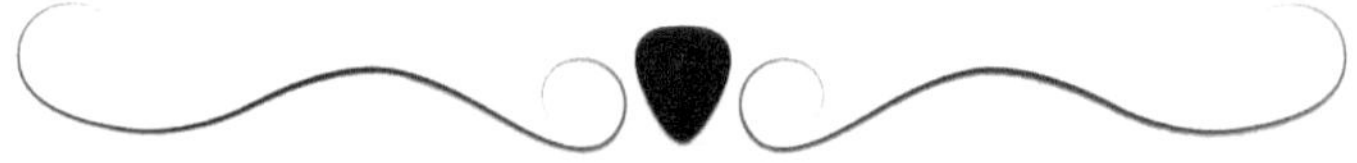

"One, two, three!" Mike clicked his drumsticks together. I shook my head furiously with Bill swinging his body back and forth. Rich nodded his head waiting for the note to come in.

It was a Saturday night and I needed this. I needed to get away and be with my boys, to remember what it was like to hold the beast of the guitar in my hands. The current that came from my fingers onto the strings gave me no better feeling than anything else in the world.

Rich moved suddenly to the mic breathing, "I try to rememberrr how we came to be / Yet all that comes to mind is miseryyy / Love is labor's lost wise man said / All that's worth remembering is what we didn't haveeee…"

I jumped up to strike the appropriate chord for the note. We finally had a couple new songs written down after what must have been months. Mike grinned at me in approval as he could see that I was really into the song. I actually wrote this one and was particularly proud. The contest in a couple months would validate my glory and honor—I could hear the cheers now.

Bill could feel it. Mike could feel it. Rich could feel it. Yet somehow, it was just innate with me even though I wasn't in the spotlight. That will change, though.

Rich growled out my last lines, "…And now you're just a distant memory / Enough to satisfy the peasant in meee…"

Bill struck his last chord and said, "Yes, break guys!"

I professed happily, saying, "We got it! That's exactly how I wanted it to sound!" I fist-pumped the air as the guys grabbed their towels.

"Yeah, it's a good one, Willoughs," Rich stated wearily. Bill took a swig of water from his bottle.

"No, this is better than good! You know what? I have an idea," I replied. "Remember Alice from the summer? She was telling me how she works at that place, Sips, a couple blocks from campus. We should perform this set over there and get a feel from an audience. Man I miss an actual stage and a crowd!" I kicked over my closed water bottle. We were practicing at Jan's boyfriend's place and it was getting too cramped for my style.

"You know, you actually haven't mentioned Alice much since last we saw her. Have you even spoken to her since?" Rich questioned. Mike and Bill leaned against the wall, clearly tired from the practice.

"Yes I have! I don't have to tell you everything that's happening in my life," I responded indignantly. I tugged at a strand of my hair. Truth was, I actually hadn't. After we left

Alice's place, I didn't even get her number. It wasn't because I didn't want to; it just didn't happen.

"Really? Because you certainly tell me everything else," Rich raised an eyebrow. "If you've spoke to her since, you wouldn't mind giving me her number so I can confirm we can perform there, right?" He glared at me, trying to catch my bluff.

"Look man, if I said I have an in, don't worry about it," I said. "I will talk to her tomorrow and let you guys know, all right?"

Rich looked at me a couple more seconds before shrugging his shoulders. "Okay then man, let us know. Bill, let's step out for a smoke."

I stood outside of the coffee shop with my hands in my pockets. It did have a homey feel like she said, almost like an imitation Starbucks with hardwood floors and rugs and paneling. The walls were made of brick and had several bookshelves line up against them. I could make out an adequate stage further inside the coffee shop and noted that there were to be several poetry slams this month.

As I calmed my nerves, I saw a few hostesses walking back and forth in white shirts, khaki pants, and brown aprons bearing Sips' logo of hands circling a coffee cup. These girls all had their hair pulled into ponytails or messy buns. I kept peering until I finally recognized Alice. As usual, she was smiling as she delivered the mugs to the customers. I wonder how she can stay so happy all the time. She didn't even seem to be working as she greeted customers, touching their shoulders, nodding to what they were saying, and almost gliding back and forth from the kitchen.

I noticed Chelsea was sitting in an armchair curled up to several textbooks and a mug of what appeared to be a cup of chai. Great, my favorite person was here. Way to boost my morale.

I sighed heavily and shook my shoulders and hands. I walked into the store to hear a bell ring marking my entrance. Immediately, I was welcomed with smooth jazz. I could discern Kenny G right away, caressing notes over his sax, and the scents of cocoa, hazelnut, and cinnamon infiltrated my senses. There were even hints of lavender as I noticed the largely female-based employees. Yet, strangely, I felt comforted by the atmosphere, like I could curl up by the window with a good Stephen King read, herbal tea, and a cat named Fluffy. Maybe I liked this place too much.

I scouted out for Alice again and saw her curly bun dip behind the counter into the kitchen area. While making my way over there, a sprite blonde popped into my field of vision with a "Tammy" name tag and said, "Hi there and welcome to Sips! Would you like a table, booth, or counter seat? I have a menu right here for ya, if you'd like. Be sure to try our new Mint 'n' Maple chai! Or even our Warm Cinnamon 'n' Tangerine latte!"

She beamed from ear to ear. Perhaps this place just has the smiling effect on its employees. "Um, I think I'll just sit at the counter if that's fine and look over the menu," I answered.

"No problem at all! If you need help with anything, please let any of our baristas know!" She smiled and spun on her heel.

I sauntered over to the counter with the menu the hostess made sure to place in my hands. Alice backed out of the kitchen door with a tray of coffees steaming and a couple of rolls.

A guy was approaching the same direction she was about to turn to head in, with his back turned as he confirmed with his girl what she wanted.

"Watch out, man!" I cautioned just as Alice turned around into the man's elbow, knocking a couple of the coffees down on the tray. The coffee reached her fingertips almost instantly, causing her to drop the tray completely from the shock of the heat.

"I am so sorry!" the man apologized sheepishly. He and I bent down to help her. I grabbed some napkins from the dispensers to soak up the coffee as he picked the rolls up off the floor.

"Crap!" she exclaimed over her fingers before turning to the guy. "Oh, it's fine. Trust me, this happens all the time. Thanks though, sir, and… Willoughs, is that you?"

"The one and only," I said through a half-smile. "You know, this is like déjà vu with you knocking over drinks. I'm not sure if the food industry is your forte."

Alice smirked. "Lucky for you, I wasn't in the same state as the other time or I could recolor your face."

"Two for two," I quickly replied.

I helped the guy pick up the tray and we placed it on the counter. The guy smiled sheepishly and walked down the counter to a different barista. I turned my face away from Alice to chuckle. "All right, Willoughs, what do you want? I'm glad your face looks better." Alice wiped her hands into her apron and started to bring the tray to the sink.

"Why must I want something? I can't visit this café and enjoy a good cup of Joe like you suggested?" I held up my hands in defense.

Alice raised an eyebrow as she dumped the contents into a nearby trash and grabbed a cloth to wipe the tray. "I don't know, Willoughs, you haven't called or said anything to me since the school year started and your friend never reached out to Chelsea either, so I'm guessing you want something." Alice placed a hand on her hip.

"Hey, when did I become the bad guy? First off, Rich and Chelsea's business is their business, and secondly, I did just help you recover from a near disaster with your orders," I defended.

Alice turned into the kitchen door shouting, "Can I get another order of caramel cappuccinos and cinnamon rolls for table eight, please?" She glanced back at me, and returned to washing the tray and dishware. "What do you want, Willoughs?"

"Okay, so here's the thing," I said. "There's this collegiate competition trying to find talent and the guys and I want to perform as much as we can in preparation for it. So we were wondering if we could do a gig or two here." I tried to put on my best face and widen my eyes. You know the ol' puppy dog routine.

Alice couldn't help but giggle at my attempt. I'm probably the farthest thing from a puppy, but anything to save face.

"I'd love to help, Willoughs, I really would, but I have no strings here to get anyone on stage. If you want a gig, you'd have to work that out with the manager, and besides, we're pretty booked since there's a poetry event this season."

"C'mon Alice, what were you saying this summer about me being to perform here?" I pleaded.

"Sorry Willoughs, it's beyond my control." Alice placed the clean tray and utensils to the side. She wiped her hands on her apron again and started back to the kitchen.

"W-wait!" I reached out to her. "Could you at least throw in a good word for me?"

"And what will I get in return?" Alice folded her arms in front of her.

"Whatever, you name it," I stated. No way was I going to let Rich think he was right.

"Hmm," Alice stepped forward, pondering my fate.

"Allie, I'm going to my room to pick up my psychology textbook, can't believe I forgot it. Do you want anything from the outside?" Chelsea adjusted her cardigan as she stepped toward our direction. When she noticed me, she nodded her head. "Sup fuckface?"

Alice glanced at me with a mischievous smile on her face and said, "I think I have the perfect favor."

Somehow I don't think Rich is going to like this.

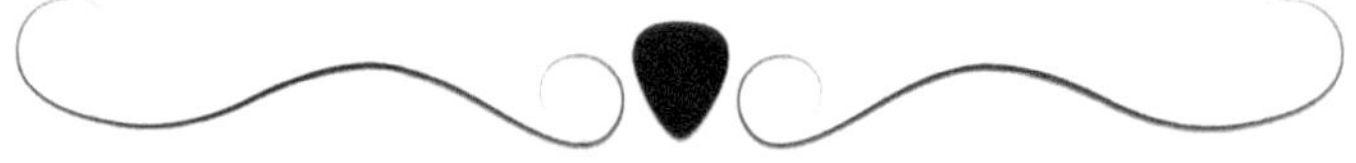

Sure enough Rich didn't.

"No man, no way! How could this be your in? You know my rule," Rich paced back and forth, wagging his finger.

It's true, he does have a rule. You see, once Rich gets what he wants from a girl or finds out something he doesn't like, he employs this No Turn Return rule. Basically when he's done, he's done. It's like the girl has served her Ultimate Purpose and then he's off to the next one. There is a reason why he's never held anyone down for long, or past a day. Or night, whichever you prefer.

"I know man, I know. But look, we have limited space and time to start performing so…" I pointed out the obvious.

"Willoughs, you don't get it man, I have only one rule. You know I'm down for anything, but this one rule is all I ask you to respect," Rich replied.

"Rich, I promise this is the only favor I'll ask of you ever again," I said. "And you know you kinda owe Chelsea. You guys didn't actually do anything from my understanding."

He told me himself. When Alice and I came back to the bath house, he and Chelsea were nowhere to be found. Later, as we got ready to leave, Rich finally came out disappointed and somewhat annoyed. He said she had fallen asleep and, furthermore, she was a virgin. I highly doubted the latter unless money was thrown at her, but if it's one thing I learned from my almost nineteen years of living, it's that you don't mess with virgins unless you're in it for the long haul. Or if you're a virgin as well.

Rich threw me an annoyed look and said, "Exactly my point. Why go out with this girl again if I'm not getting anything more than a feel?"

"Rich my man, what happened to the old Casanova you?" I playfully punched his jaw. "You can get any girl you want, no worries. All rules have exceptions and it's college, people act differently when they're cold and lonely. Plus, she's hot and a really sweet girl." Okay, I probably stretched the truth on that last part. Rich shook his head but I could tell he was getting his ego back.

"Willoughs, you owe me one. So when is this date?"

"Tonight," I said as I scratched my head.

"What?!" Rich shouted.

"Yeah, actually in like a couple hours," I stated.

Rich nodded his head. "Oh yeah, when I need a favor from you, it is going to be sooo good. So good." Rich turned on his heel and started undressing for a shower.

"Never you mind about that, Rich. Worry about making this date the night of her life, you dog you!" I jested.

Rich chuckled to himself as he grabbed his towel.

I might regret this later.

So the date went well for the most part. Rich did his part in making the date the best it could be. He acted like a gentleman, pulling out her chair, opening the car door, the whole nine yards. Chelsea even let him go a little further than a feel. The only downside to the date—we're now out of a singer.

Rich coughed into the phone and said, "Look man, you're going to owe me so much so I guess this week you're going to have to either sing yourself or perform acoustics of our songs. I won't be better for at least another week."

Apparently, Chelsea had just gotten over the flu and somehow passed it on to Rich. All this and finally we got an in and a gig at Alice's place this week. I even had to move down the hall to Bill and Mike's dorm since Rich was hacking up his lungs the past couple of nights since the date. Great.

Angel I. Hawkins

None of the rest of us could sing and who wants to hear acoustics of songs they don't even know? We may as well perform at a funeral. A band is only as good as its lead singer, and without Rich, we're screwed. Bill and Mike sound like cats when they try to sing, and though I can hold a tune, no one comes to listen to me. Rich has the voice and the presence.

Hanging up the phone, I decided to visit the library to look at the book Dr. Belk had on reserve for the class.

I left the dorm building and turned left. It was a little colder now that November was here. I pulled my hood over my head and noticed there were less people on the lawn. Those who were there were in what appeared to be study groups or couples cuddling on the tree swings.

I passed a few buildings until I came upon a crowd of students. The huddled mass was so thick I could hardly make out what the center of the commotion was. I peered up and surprisingly, a few members of the crowd were taller than me.

I turned to my right and nudged this black guy in the shoulder. "Hey, what's all this about?"

He rolled his eyes at me and turned back to the center of attention. "Preach, Dwayne!" I looked back to the center and could finally make out the center of attention.

"Brothers and sisters! How long must we fight before we get better treatment here? How long must we endure the strains of financial aid through loans? How long must we worry whether we'll get a job after college? How long must we wonder whether the four-year degree is truly worth it?" a dark-skinned man I'm supposing is Dwayne bellowed on the steps of the student lounge.

He was dressed smartly with a navy blue suit and an African hat of kente cloth. He wore a light mink shawl over his shoulders and his spectacles shone brightly as he spoke his words. There was a black girl standing next to him with pin curls and a deep blue shirt and skirt. She had red lipstick on and a sad expression on her face. There was another girl on his left but she was so tiny I could hardly make her out. Another black guy stood behind them. He was light-skinned with green eyes and a crisp white shirt tucked into black slacks. He wore a huge leather jacket and nodded in agreement to what Dwayne was saying.

I noticed I was surrounded by black people, with a handful of white faces and more than a handful of Hispanics. I have honestly never been in such a diverse space and it almost frightened me.

Dwayne started again saying, "Brothers and sisters, if we want change, we have to stick together! We have to be organized to have fairer treatment and act as one! We can't sit idly by hoping for change, neither can we act too rash. If we want more aid in the form of scholarships and if we want to have better professional opportunities, we have to put in the work, too! Brothers and sisters, hear me out."

"Yes, you go Dwayne!" another voice shouted.

Several people shook their heads and clapped in approval. I rolled my eyes. Yet no matter that I was getting slightly bored, there was something in the way he commanded the crowd. He was almost regal-like. His voice demanded attention and its deep tenor begged to be heard. Even his posse seemed to know of this and couldn't move from their stance. I was curious, though, of who was next to Dwayne as the person was so short I still couldn't make her out. I decided to turn to my left and I nudged a black girl, asking her, "What group is this? What is this for?"

"This is Ubuntu, a student organization that welcomes all races to discuss and advocate for issues involving students, the community, or whatever you think is important," she answered, then pointed at the speaker. "And that's Dwayne. He's the student president. We're having this demonstration based on some concerns from several of our members of how they were denied more financial aid and are at risk of dropping out since they can't afford to continue attending."

"Fascinating. What does Ubuntu mean? And who are his posse, like the vice president and whatnot?" I inquired.

The girl, seemingly pleased that I was so interested, replied, "Well Ubuntu comes from South Africa and means "human-ness" or basically, humanity. Those people you see standing around Dwayne, though, are some members of the student board. The girl in the blue next to him is our vice president and his girlfriend. The guy behind them is our secretary and the short girl is the treasurer, although she also seems to advocate for things as well."

I nodded to her and said, "Thanks."

"You should come to our meetings. We have one every other Tuesday in Miller Hall from 5-7 p.m." She blinked at me.

Uh-oh. See, I was never into extracurriculars even in high school, let alone consider joining one in college. To me, it's like a waste of time, you know? Why spend time outside of class with people you barely tolerate inside of class?

Before I could explain this reasoning to her, someone whispered to us, "Shush!"

We looked over to Dwayne, who continued, "Brothers and sisters, if you are interested in our movement or want to learn more about this organization, there are interest forms circulating around. It would behoove you to sign up even if you would just want to join our e-mail list." Behoove. Listen to this guy, who uses that word anymore? That's the kind of thing that would make me not want to join a student organization. The girl seemed invested in what he was saying, so using that as my cue, I started to slowly back away from the throng.

Dwayne continued. "Thank you all for listening. Our very own Alice Atkins will close with a hymn to lift your spirits, so please be respectful."

The mention of Alice piqued my interest and made me stop in my tracks. Dwayne handed her the mic and instantly I knew who the short person was standing beside him the whole time. She didn't even need the mic, though, because as soon as he gave it to her, her voice filled the space.

Her voice was warm and inviting just as her skin was. It was irresistible and brought others in.

"I sing because I'm happy…His eye was oonnn the sparrowww, and I knowwww He watches, watches me…!!" she sang.

There was so much emotion in each word that had the misfortune to leave her mouth. You couldn't leave her if you tried. She had such range that she could sing low and then reach the highest falsetto. She alternated from the extremes and back again. She played with her voice, teasing us and our ears with her magic. I could feel the seriousness in her voice and could feel the moments I was certain she was smiling. I tried standing on my tiptoes to fully appreciate the experience, but gave up and decided to enjoy the moment. When she finished her last note, I knew we had found our temporary singer.

"You know, Willoughs, you ask a lot of favors," Alice said. I had finally gotten her to agree to fill in for Rich on the condition he took Chelsea out again. Man she seems set on that hookup. We were standing outside of the garage where Bill and Mike were waiting. I hadn't even told them of my brilliant plan yet. "Do the guys even know that I'm filling in?" Alice asked the very thing on my mind.

"Not exactly," I hesitated.

"Willoughs!" Alice hissed. She punched my arm, rather hard I might add. My coloring was back to normal and I couldn't afford any more bruises.

"Hey hey hey, relax!" I hissed back, rubbing my arm. "They have no choice but to let you since Rich got sick from your friend!"

Alice ran her hand through her curls. "Willoughs, I don't know."

"What is there not to know? The guys like you well enough," I reasoned. "Let me warm them up and then you wow them. We're going to need someone since we're on a time crunch and it'll be an interesting sound."

Alice looked at me doubtfully and said, "Fine. Whether or not they go through with this, Rich still has to give Chelsea a chance."

"I got you, I got you," I reassured her. I was racking so many IOU's lately, I needed to keep a tab. I bent down to pull the garage door up and placed my arm around Alice. I may as well have put my hand on my own hip, she was so tiny. "Fellas, I have our solution!" Alice groaned under my arm.

Bill and Mike looked up from their instruments to take in the scene, puzzled. Mike adjusted his beanie and shouted out, "Well hello, Alice, long time no see!"

"Hey Alice," Bill nodded and reciprocated.

Alice smiled. "Hey guys."

"So what do you mean you found our solution? I thought we were going to do acoustics," Bill asked as he turned to me.

Alice wriggled from under my arm and found herself a seat not too far from the guys and their instruments. She crossed her legs and folded her arms, looking at me to see how I was going to repair this.

I walked steadily toward the guys and said, "Are we performing for a nursing home, guys? No. What we need is a singer!" I lifted my index finger as if to make a point. Bill and Mike glanced at each other.

Mike started, "Let me guess, are you going to sing, Willoughs?" Bill and Mike snickered to themselves.

"You flatter me, Mike." I clasped my hands and walked over to Alice. "But alas, no, the world is not ready for my magnificence. No sir, Alice will have to be our new singer until Rich feels better." I placed my hands on her shoulders in finality.

Bill and Mike glanced at each other, unsure. "Willoughs, can we deliberate over here?" Bill asked.

"Excuse us a second," Mike said to Alice. Alice nodded her head in understanding.

Mike pulled my forearm to the side out of earshot of Alice and lowered his voice saying, "Is Rich okay with this? I don't mind too much but..."

"Yeah, what did he say? She only listened in on one of our gigs. We have a particular sound, you know," Bill continued. "I'm sure she may sound nice and all but getting a new singer changes the band."

"Don't you think I know this? Listen, if you heard her sing, you'd know that she could definitely take on our sound," I explained. "She has range and I think she could definitely take over in the meantime."

"But did you ask Rich?" Mike asked again. "If he finds an outsider took his place, he might not be too happy about that." Bill shook his head, seemingly worried as well.

"I don't think Rich would mind at all, he'll more than likely thank me!" I shrugged. "Plus everyone knows that you don't do acoustics on your first night anywhere. I'll deal with him when the time is right. Hey, maybe when he's better, they can do a duet to ease him back as our front man!"

Bill and Mike looked at each other over this suggestion. Even I surprised myself with it as I said it. That would be something. I turned to Alice, winked, and gave her the OK sign. Alice shook her head and smiled.

"Well, Willoughs, you're going to have to break this to Rich when he feels better," Mike said and walked back to his drums. Bill raised his eyebrows, crossed his arms, and made his way over to his guitar.

"Welcome to the band, Alice!" I opened my arms.

It turns out, I was more than right about Alice. She fit in like a glove. Her voice almost fit in better than Rich's and she gave our sound more soul than Rich's raspiness could muster. Not only that, but she was a performer. Her body writhed smoothly against the microphone, yet she could rock out with the best of them. She memorized our set in no time and was able to perform as if she had been a part of our band since the beginning of time.

As we got our equipment ready and set up in the coffee house for our first gig, Alice stepped in with her hair pinned into a curly almost-Mohawk. She sported silver pumps and black leggings with a black leather jacket. She wore a silver beaded bandeau showcasing her flat stomach and more swallow tattoos on her side. Mike and I raised our eyebrows at the sight of her.

"Well? Or is it too much?" Alice raised her shoulders in question.

"You look perfect," Mike said, enveloping her in his gaze.

"Willoughs?" Alice asked again, twirling around so I could get the full effect.

"Well, now you could say you're up to my chest," I replied matter-of-factly. Seriously, her heels were sky high. Hopefully she doesn't have another clumsy accident.

Alice rolled her eyes and started pushing the chairs into a structured seating format.

Mike hit my chest and said, "Dude?"

I hit him back on his arm and repeated, "Dude?" Mike

shook his head and went back to his drums.

Bill walked into the café. "Nice guys! It feels so homey in here! Nice look, Alice!" He rubbed his crossed arms as he made way to his guitar.

"Thanks," Alice smiled.

The coffee shop was temporarily closed as we set up. Turns out, the perky blonde who greeted me the other week was the manager, so there wasn't much persuasion needed for us to have the coffee shop. Showtime was in a couple more hours and with their clientele, we were expected to have a decent audience. My nerves were getting some adrenaline as I anticipated the new crowd. I don't get nervous, but excited, when performing someplace new and couldn't wait to debut our music.

Rich still thought we were doing acoustics with me singing on a couple songs. It wasn't a complete lie. We would have acoustics, you know, accompanied by some singing. Or a lot of singing, however you would prefer to say it.

"Yeah, I like the vibe here," Mike agreed. "It's like being in a coffee-filled Bath 'n' Body Works!"

"Hey, do you guys want any coffee or tea or any pastries?" Alice asked from the other side of the room as she neared the counter.

"I'll have an iced coffee, black," Mike replied.

"I'll have one of those oatmeal cookies, if that's fine," Bill offered.

"I'm good," I replied.

"Coming right up, then," Alice turned and walked into the kitchen.

"You guys ready?" Bill asked, rubbing his hands together. I could tell his nerves were starting. While I got excited to perform at new places, Bill was the opposite. He got nervous until he was used to a place. Too bad Rich wasn't here to go out for a smoke with him and calm his nerves.

Mike, knowing this, took a cue and placed his hands on Bill's shoulders. "Look man, we're going to be great. You like this place already, so we'll be good."

Bill nodded his head. "I'm fine, I swear. I just wish Rich was here. I think he might like Alice and think he would like our sound. I like her, Willoughs."

"Yeah I do, too," Mike said as he looked at me. I gave a half-smile. I found myself liking her, too.

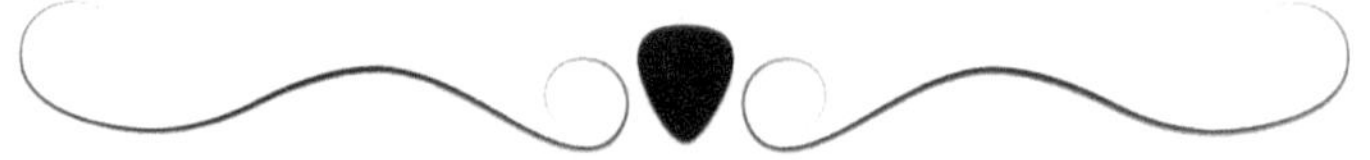

So everything was going well. We opened well and the crowd was more than decent, as promised. Alice controlled the crowd and they loved our sound. In the middle of about the fourth song, right before we were to have an intermission, Rich walked in. He had a thick scarf around his neck and a wool beanie. His nose was red and his face seemed a bit puffy.

I was the first to notice him and looked to Bill and Mike, but they were in their zone. I looked to Alice, but either she was feeling the song too much or she didn't much care who was in the audience. Rich made his way to a seat next to the counter and put his hand to chin as if critiquing our performance. Chelsea was closer to the stage and was smiling and for once was swaying to something we produced. Hopefully their reunion doesn't suffer because of this.

Then, instead of letting it bother me or get to me as things tend to do, I just decided to turn back to my guitar and rock out. I closed my eyes and let Alice's voice and our instrument sounds mingle. I let them smooth over and crash into my ears. My fingers followed suit over the chords. I stomped my foot in rhythm to our sound and could feel droplets of sweat coming down my face, from my forehead to my nose to my chin. The music guided them off my face. Some fell onto my hands. Some onto my chest. Some onto my guitar. But nothing else mattered for those few moments.

Yet sooner than I knew it, Alice stepped to the microphone and breathed, "I'd like to thank all of you for supporting the band Left Red Door. We're going to have a little intermission right now, but I just wanted to point out the actual lead singer of this band who I'm filling in for, Rich! He's sitting right there at the counter, but wasn't feeling well enough to perform today and still managed to come out! Rich, wave to these lovely folks!" She pointed her hand in his direction, sweat pulsing from her temples. The crowd's eyes followed where she was pointing.

Rich, a little taken aback, waved to the crowd. Everyone applauded and smiled in encouragement. Getting his ego back from the support, he stood up and nodded and bowed before the bows took too much from him and he doubled over coughing. The crowd laughed in appreciation of this and turned to us, applauding some more. Chelsea ran over to Rich's aid and rubbed his back, handing him tissues. Rich looked up from her and gave us a half-smile.

He was soon able to straighten himself out and smile full-force, clapping at us. He beamed. Perhaps we would be getting a new addition after all.

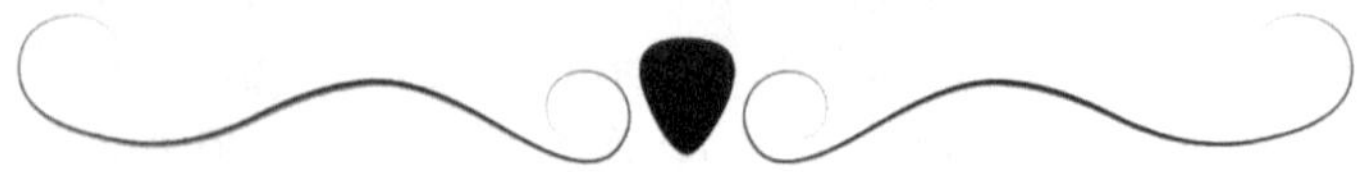

"What we should do is create a petition!"

"No, let's write a letter to the University president!"

"Maybe we should storm in front of the financial aid office?"

"How about we get everyone to not attend their classes?"

"…Yeah, we should totally do that!"

"Yeah!"

The back and forth of the suggestions was making me feel invigorated. I could feel the passion of the students. Also, I was totally down for the skipping-out-on-class bit. Physics was kicking my ass so hard.

"Here, here! Settle down people!" Dwayne hit the podium with the mallet and said, "We have to attend classes because we paid for it! What's the matter with you all? Now the other suggestions seem valid. Let's get the letter started, and let's organize the appearance at financial aid!"

"Dwayne, man, I don't have time to be waiting idly and playing nice with these people," one guy pleaded. "I'm working three jobs to help make up for what my loans don't cover and it's still not enough. We need action! We need to leave a mark!"

"Sure do!" someone else agreed in the back.

I raised my eyebrows to Alice, but she seemed invested in the seeming radicals. She leaned forward in her chair, face set in a serious expression as she heard out their concerns.

"How is it that I got a 2300 on my SAT, and my classmate got an 1800, mind you a white classmate, and he has a full scholarship? What kind of crap is that?" another questioned. This person stood up in the circle and turned around for everyone to see. She was a heavier girl, slightly darker than Alice with a natural buzz cut. "I have maintained a 4.0 GPA throughout my time here and every time I go to see someone about it, nothing gets done. They say, 'Sorry, we can't help you' or 'we only give scholarships to incoming freshmen' or 'maybe we'll have something in the fall.' Pssh, yeah right!" The room exploded in clapping and commotion over her predicament. I felt genuinely shocked. I got a 1750 and only a partial scholarship. Maybe I should ask her about that classmate.

"Not to downplay anyone else's situation or try to exploit anyone, but what about those who, yeah may be well off, but don't get any funding? I worked my butt off in high school, and though my parents may have some money, that doesn't mean they were necessarily going to pay for my education," another girl stood up. She was lighter skinned with hair down to her butt. The room silenced a bit as if questioning the significance of her plight. "My parents are doctors, but they had to work to get where they were going and they expected the same of me. I graduated top of my class, high SAT scores, after school activities, everything, and I didn't get anything!"

"Then why did she come here?" I whispered to Alice. Alice elbowed my rib, annoyed. "Shh!"

"...Look, we all have stories here and no matter your background or financial status, you should receive aid based on your merits and nothing else!" the girl reasoned. The other students nodded their heads in agreement. Some clapped their hands in support.

"Brothers and sisters, our family all makes valid points. The amount the school charges and the fact that this is a private university, meaning funding comes from outside sources, means there should be more money to give to our students. You work hard and you choose to attend this university for whatever reason, and the university should keep your best interests at heart," Dwayne stated. "The university would be nothing without its students and our rights dictate that if we are not satisfied with something, we have the right to try and change it. This is a continual cycle that happens. If the students are happy, they would be more willing to donate back to their alma mater making sure others are happy, but if there is unrest, that only brings problems to the university."

Alice seemed to absorb his words. She stood up and clapped full-force, as did several other members at that moment. I agreed with what he was saying, but something wasn't sitting right with me and I couldn't put my finger on it. Nevertheless, I clapped lightly. I looked at Dwayne and noticed he had such a somber look on his face. He looked tired, but like he knew he had an obligation to his members.

His vice president stood next to him wearing the same expression. The secretary guy was sitting nearby at the opening of the circle. Alice and I were sitting on the sideline of the circle. At first, I was hesitant about actually attending a meeting, but with the students' passion and conviction in their stories, you couldn't help but feel something for them.

It was true. How could someone smarter and more involved get barely anything for their efforts as opposed to someone who had subpar or mediocre efforts? I wasn't the brightest bulb in high school, did not have any extracurriculars, and got an average SAT (or I like to flatter myself calling it average), but nonetheless, I received an adequate package to attend Ridgewood. My parents didn't have to worry much about my funding and if I wanted extra cash, I worked, which I did but that wasn't out of extreme necessity, but rather want. I couldn't even imagine working more than two jobs to make ends meet. I was struggling to keep up with the job I had, for goodness' sake. Forget it if I had children as a handful of the members here had. It's scary becoming an adult.

I noticed some members who had told their stories had tears streaming down their faces as others tried to console them, rubbing their shoulders or just letting them cry. But really, how could you console that?

Alice soon plopped down into her chair, pumped from the revelation. She whispered to me, "Hey, thanks for coming. It means a lot for others to hear these stories. If nothing else, we need to spread the awareness of what's going on, you know?"

"Yeah, no problem. I love this stuff, activism, whoo!" I put my fists in the air. Alice chuckled before pulling my arms down. I threw a half-smile in her direction which made her turn away. I don't know if it was the excitement of the evening or what, but she was definitely blushing, if that's possible.

"Well brothers and sisters, it's about time to wrap up," Dwayne started. "We'll be passing around a sign-in sheet for those interested in helping construct and mail out letters. Those who want to help out with the demonstration should sign the green sheet, and if anyone is interested in joining our lovely committees, we will need dedicated members. Let's see, any other announcements?"

His second in command came forward. "Yes, remember we are helping out at St. Matthew's Church at the soup kitchen, serving food this coming Saturday. There will also be a gift wrapping event the following Thursday from 3-5 p.m. If anyone is interested, we will need about five more members to take part in that. Other than that, thanks all for coming, and new members. Oh Dwayne, you forgot!" She tapped him lightly on his shoulder. Dwayne rubbed his sweaty face with a cloth draped from his shoulder.

"Oh yes! Do we have any visitors and/or new members with us today?" Dwayne remembered. About seven people stood up, causing Alice to nudge me in the ribs. She really needs to stop doing that. I stood up at her cue and everyone clapped for us, smiling as if welcoming fresh meat.

"Thank you all for coming and we hope that, if nothing else today, we've inspired you to take notice of the little things that go on with yourself and fellow classmates in this institution," Dwayne said. "We aim to educate here as well and firmly believe in the old saying, 'If you know better, you do better,' ain't that right, brothers and sisters?" The members clapped in agreement. Dwayne continued, "Before you sit down, would you mind sharing your name and how you came about spending the evening with us?"

What is this, fifth grade?

"Evan, and I saw the demonstration the other week and thought I'd stop by."

"Margaret, and I saw the flyer near the library."

"Alicia, and Devon always said I should stop by, so here I am."

Others filled in their mini introductions. Evan and I were the only new white guys there. In fact, there were probably no more than ten white people in the meeting. Interesting.

"Willoughs, and I owed Alice here," I stated matter-of-factly and then promptly sat down. A couple of the members looked at each other. I noticed the secretary guy looking over, intrigued by us.

"Well, welcome to Ubuntu, and if you'd like to become a full member, there is a one-time fee of $10. You can sign in with our secretary and he'll fill you in on what we do here or you could always ask our members," Dwayne said. "If you decide to become a full member, we encourage you to be an active participant. It's not enough to be a part of humanity if our members aren't being treated as such and we use every effort to strive to the meaning of our name. Thanks for coming." This closing remark sparked everyone to gather their coats and bags. Some smiled and nodded in my direction. A couple people came over to shake my hand as Alice made her way to the podium with a folder and several large envelopes.

"Thanks for coming, man," a couple guys patted my back on their way out.

"My pleasure," I reassured. Someone passed me the sign-in sheets and a pen. I contemplated for a minute. There was a symbol of a heart with red, black, and green coloring on the inside. How original. I sighed as I jotted down my information on the sign-in sheets—wouldn't hurt to get more spam e-mail. I looked to my left to pass the sheets and saw a couple people talking with the secretary.

He stood erect and dressed smartly, again with a blue suit this time and a red bowtie and brown pointed alligator shoes. Gosh, I hate guys who wear stuff like that. Bowties have to be the most annoying invention ever. Like seriously, what's the point? As if regular ties weren't bad enough, someone decided to make guys' lives even harder with those prissy things. And that's another thing, only uppity people wear those stupid monstrosities as if to make a point that they accomplished folding and tying it. He nodded at the students' inquiries with feigned interest. His eyes shifted every now and then to Alice. It was something in the way he kept looking at her that irked me. Or maybe it was how he was dressed. Perhaps both. Again, something rubbed me wrong with this setting.

I walked up to him as the other two people departed. "Bye Chester, see you next week, thanks so much!"

I snickered to myself. What a load of baloney. Who names their kid Chester? That's like asking to be made fun of.

"Hey, Williams, right?" Chester acknowledged. He put on a fake, yet brilliantly white smile, as if he's done this hundreds of times before. He stretched his hand to shake mine.

"Willoughs," I corrected before shaking his hand and faking my own smile. I know too many guys like this.

"Willoughs, my, that's an interesting name. It's usually a last name, correct?" Chester blinked.

"Uh-huh. Look, I was wondering if I could pay my dues to be a full member like Dwayne was saying," I replied. Chester looked me up and down before managing up his notebook from his traveler's bag and envelope.

"Right," he said. "That'll be $10, one-time fee. I will need you to fill out your information here and we will place you on our mailing list for our announcements and events…"

"Gotcha," I said before he could continue. He raised an eyebrow at me before he handed me the notebook. He turned to get some flyers and brochures and procured an envelope as I filled in my information.

"Well, if you have any questions, you are welcome to get in contact with any of us here," Chester stated.

"Thanks. I'll be sure to do that," I replied and pulled a

$10 bill.

"Welcome," Chester said before flashing another bright smile. There were crinkles around his eyes when he smiled. I heard some chicks say they dig that, and that it makes the guys look more mature and sophisticated. Of course he would have that. And what was up with everyone having such great and dazzling teeth. I needed to visit their dentists.

He held out his hand for me to shake again, but there was just something so inauthentic in it. I shook his hand as Alice came over to us. "Hey, Willoughs, I see you've met Chester!" She smiled from him to me.

"Yeah, Willoughs here just decided to join Ubuntu," Chester lit up. His demeanor changed suddenly. His smile felt more real and he placed a hand on her shoulder.

"Great, Willoughs. I didn't know you enjoyed the meeting that much," Alice noted, seeming surprised. Chester's hand moved around her shoulder and his eyes turned warm. I noticed how very brown they looked.

"Yeah well, you've done a lot for the band and I lately, so I figured why not? And it seems like a good way to get involved," I shrugged.

"Band?" Chester remembered I was standing there. "Do you sing? We could actually use more singers or instrumentalists, if you're interested." Poor guy, pretending to actually care.

"I play guitar and have some pretty good chops, if I do say so myself," I smirked. "But I'll get back to you on that."

"Hey, any way you can help out, brother," Chester stated.

"Yeah, you don't have to feel pressured to do anything. I saw you signed up for our other events and we could use any help you're willing to offer," Alice reassured.

My phone rang at that moment and, noting it was a call from Bill, and thanking goodness I was saved from yet another obligation, I placed my hand on Alice's wrist closest to me. "I understand and will definitely think about it. Uh, Alice it's about time we go. Bill is calling for us."

"Oh, right," Alice remembered. "Chester, I'll see you next week, right?" She turned to give him a hug and a kiss on the cheek.

"Definitely," he murmured into her curls. I actually don't remember her ever giving me a hug. I let the phone go to voicemail as she went to get her coat and bags.

"Nice meeting you, Willoughs," Chester nodded to me as he collected his own materials.

"Likewise," I replied dryly.

Chester gathered his materials and turned to leave, traveler's bag on his shoulder and mink in his arm. Yeah, something isn't right with that kid.

"Okay, ready when you are," Alice chirped.

"Hey Alice, can I ask you something?" I wondered.

"Sure, what's up?" Alice gazed up at me as we made our way to the exit.

"You and Chester, have you guys ever…?" I asked, almost questioning where I was going with this.

"Have we ever what?" Alice continued, seeming to egg me on to spit it out.

"W-well you know, have you guys went out? Do you two have a history?" I finally uttered, as I held open the door. The brisk cold swept us as we stepped outside. Fall would soon be ending, I could tell.

"Hmm, wouldn't you like to know?" Alice replied coyly. She sprinted up to her car at the end of the parking lot.

"What kind of reply is that? I'm asking for a reason," I huffed as I picked up my pace to catch up with the pixie.

"I think the better question is, why does it matter? What difference does it make if Chester and I went out or not?" Alice replied as she stepped up into her car.

Why was she making this so difficult? It was a simple question. Why does there have to be strings attached? I wished I could say this, but a bigger part of me knew why I needed to know the answer. I walked around the other side of the car and climbed in. I never understood the reasoning behind small women and big cars. The leather interior gave off that new car smell that I loved. I fastened my seatbelt and held onto the flyers Chester had given me.

"I guess it doesn't make a difference," I said.

"Suit yourself," Alice shrugged as she dipped her key into the ignition. I looked over at her as she moved her steering wheel and started to back out of the parking space. She pushed for her radio to start playing, and soon, Lauryn Hill's aching vocals wafted the car.

I turned halfway to her and started again sincerely. "It does make a difference if you're seeing him or not. I get a bad vibe from that guy and I really don't think he's the guy for you." I tried looking into her eyes even though she had her eyes on the road.

"What do you mean? Chester's one of the sweetest guys I know!" Alice proclaimed. "I think you might be a smidge intimidated. He can certainly sport a bowtie." I could tell she was teasing me with the last bit.

I feigned a gagging reflex. "Please, anyone who's anyone knows that bowties are basically the definition of arrogance." I snorted and rolled my eyes to the window. "Besides who wear that and alligator shoes and mink? Who does he think he is? Only old guys wear that shit."

"Willoughs, oh my gosh!" Alice exclaimed, amused. "You're so jealous!"

"Am not!" I replied indignantly.

"Are too!" Alice wagged her finger chuckling. "But seriously, Chester is a good guy. We grew up together and he really is one of the nicest guys I know. You should give him a chance. You can't fault the man because he likes to dress a certain way."

"I don't know, Alice, there's just something about him and it's not just the way he dresses," I muttered. Alice glanced at me for a split second before turning back to the road, smirking.

"Yeah, well, if you come to more meetings since you're a full paid member, you'll see," Alice said.

We came to a stop sign and Alicia Keys wailed through the radio. My phone rang again showing my mom was calling.

"Hey mom," I picked up.

"Hey Will-oohs!!" Ella breathed into the phone.

"Ella-Bella, what's up?" my face instantly lit up. Alice noted this and gave a polite smile.

"Nothing much, Will-oohs, when you coming home?" Ella pleaded.

"Soon soon, Ella-Bella, in about three weeks for Christmas if you can wait that long," I said, although knowing full well she didn't yet have a grasp on time.

"Three weeks? You'll be home in no time!" Ella perked. I heard muffling in the background and could make out my mother bargaining with Ella over the phone. Kids, I mouthed to Alice. Alice giggled.

"Willoughs, honey, is there anything you'd like for Christmas?" my mother finally got a hold of the phone. "Your father and I saw your mid-term marks and are glad you're holding up over there. Just make sure to turn that C around in calculus!" I could hear the familiar worrying of my mother on the other end of the receiver.

"It is very much noted," I sighed into the phone.

"Is that music I hear in the background? You should be studying, Willoughs, we want nothing less than B's and we mean it!" my mother stated. "And don't be drinking and driving and…"

"Yeah I got it, ma," I replied.

"Willoughs, are you at a party?" my mother inquired.

"No, mom, far from it. I'm riding over to practice with Alice," I stated, simply. Alice perked up when I mentioned her name.

"Alice? That's the same girl who joined your little group, right? You're spending an awful amount of time with her lately," my mother observed. Way to state the obvious, Mom.

"Yes, mom," I felt myself blushing.

"If you're spending that much time together, you might want to consider inviting her over for Christmas dinner," Mom continued.

"Mom, I'm sure she has things to do for Christmas besides hanging out with us," I lowered my voice into the phone.

"What's that you say, Willoughs? I can hardly hear you. Put Alice on the phone. It's only a dinner, she doesn't have to stay the whole day," Mom said.

"Mom!" I raised my voice a little.

"Willoughs, don't use that tone with me, now put her on the phone!" my mother commanded.

Alice had an amused look on her face at my reaction. Everything okay? she mouthed. I gave a sheepish smile and nodded before saying, "Yeah uh, my mom wanted to speak with you."

Alice faked surprise by clutching her chest before she started giggling and took the phone. "Hello, Mrs. Willoughs!" She had a bright smile on as if she were talking to my mom face-to-face. She kept driving with her hand on the wheel and soon we were pulling up to the garage for practice.

Every so often she would laugh and nod, turning to me every few seconds. She held up a finger as if to say a minute more, as my mind scrambled of all the embarrassing things my mother could say.

"I actually wouldn't mind coming over for dinner. I won't be able to stay too long since my dad will be having some council members over to the house," Alice explained. "Mmmhmm yeah, my dad is Councilman Atkins…Yes, THE Councilman Atkins…It's no problem really, they see me every year…"

I half hoped my mother would see this as intrusive and that she couldn't possibly tear Alice away from her family. Then again, a part of me wanted my family to meet her. I was pretty sure they would like Alice. What's not to like, right?

"…Great, it was really nice speaking with you. Uh-huh, I look forward to seeing you then," Alice began to wrap up. "And I will be sure to tell my father that. You take care now. Would you like to speak with Willoughs again? Okay, bye now." She hung up the phone and handed it back to me, "Your mom seems like such a darling!" She grinned from ear to ear.

"Thanks, I'll be sure to put that in the Christmas card," I started to unbuckle my seatbelt.

Alice held out her hand, stopping me from exiting the car, "Wait, Willoughs, you don't mind, right? I only accepted because I couldn't say no to her on the phone, but I don't want you to feel uncomfortable." She looked at me seriously, asking permission with her round brown doe eyes.

Her eyes were huge, I noticed now. I could smell her now that she was close to me. With something of cocoa and sandalwood, she smelled as pretty as she looked. Her hair was pulled into a ponytail on top with the rest of her curly ringlets hanging down past her shoulders. Her cheeks held signs of dimples and her full lips seemed glossier than ever.

I guess I stared at her a little too long as she sat back into her seat, keeping her eyes on me, matching my intensity, almost daring me to do something. Her arm had moved from across my chest onto my arm that laid on the armrest closest to her. I looked down at her petite hands and noticed nicely manicured white nails from her smooth-looking rich mocha hands. They looked so warm and inviting.

I took her hand into my own and rubbed my thumb on top of it. Her hands were so soft and light, it was as if I was holding silk. I placed my fingers between hers and noted the differences. My skin was so pale compared to hers and so huge, yet her hand seemed to just fit into mine like a glove. I turned her hand over, palm facing upward. I knew I was stalling now, but I never fully recognized or was even able to revel in just touching her.

I could feel her eyes boring into my neck, waiting for a verbal response or something more than my playing with her hand. I hardly dared looking into her eyes, knowing what I should do and wondering how to go about it. I finally managed to croak, "Of course I don't mind you coming over. I think I'd mind more if I didn't see you." I looked up finally at the last part.

Her eyes softened, as if they couldn't do more damage to my chest. Her face slowly turned into a half-smile and she blinked. I raised my other hand to place on her cheek when Mike pulled up the garage door, blinding us with the light from inside the garage and forcing us to turn away from each other, as if nothing happened.

"I thought I saw headlights. Man, what took you both so long?" Mike walked over, hands outstretched and oblivious to what almost happened. "Hurry up guys, we've been here for almost an hour waiting. Let's get moving." Mike clapped his hands as if to rush us along.

Alice gave a half-smile as she unbuckled her seatbelt. "Well I'm glad I accepted, then. And to answer your question from before, Chester and I never dated." The mere mention of Chester snapped me back even more into the present.

Alice hopped out of the car and walked up to Mike arms outstretched as well. "We're here, Mike! Now, as much as you make us wait for practice…" Mike scooped her into a full bear hug and picked her up, spinning her around causing her to shriek in delight while tapping him to put her down. Bill and Rich were further inside talking about something or other. I smiled at the sight and bounded from the car as well. Chester-0, me-1.

Winter.

"**W**illoughs, now you put on that sweater Aunt Bertha gave you!" mom yelled from upstairs.

"Ma!" I yelled back, annoyed. It was the most God-awful sweater a family member could give you. It was this woolly red sweater with blue bows protruding at odd angles on the sweater and green ribbons streaming from every which way. There were presents sewn into the sweater of different shapes and white stitching reading, Someone who loves me gave me this sweater. I think the stitching got that wrong; no one who loved me would ever give me this sweater. Seriously, this sweater redefined the ugly sweater, and my mom wanted me to wear this in front of company?

"Don't make me come up there. Bertha spent a lot of time making that sweater for you, so put it on and let me take a picture!" mom demanded.

"Yeah Willoughs, let us see it," I heard Rich shout up. I could hear the smirk in his voice. Great, so company was already here. I looked at the card that accompanied the sweater reading:

"With love, your Aunt Bertha, wear this sweater in good health!"

Geez, the material even made me itch. I noticed several pieces of thread coming out of the sweater. With my luck, maybe the sweater would just come apart when the flash struck it from the camera. I sighed and tugged the sweater down over my head. I glanced in the mirror and noticed the sweater fit a little baggily over my frame.

As I made my way downstairs, I noticed Dad sitting back in his favorite chair watching TV while Ella played not too far from him on the floor with her new dolls. Rich was sitting in an opposite chair from my dad texting who knows who, and Mom was in the kitchen.

"Ta-da," I offered half-heartedly.

Rich put his hand to his mouth in mild shock, "Oh Willoughs, that is the best!"

Dad looked back and then quickly turned to the TV again trying to hide his smile. "Looks good, Willoughs!"

Ella smiled the brightest. "Ooh, Will-oohs! I love your sweater, I want one!"

Upon hearing these exclamations, Mom rushed in, teetering on her two-inch heels and long wool skirt. "Willoughs, this is absolutely darling! We have to include this in the Christmas card and send it to Bertha. She's going to be so happy! Now make sure you call her and thank her for this lovely sweater!"

These people have got to be kidding me. I put on my best smile as Mom took her pictures. After she had finished and ran back to the kitchen to check on the food, Dad came up to me handing me $20. "For your troubles, son. We all have to put up with something, but we've never had to put up with that." He patted me on the back as he gave a full laugh going up the stairs. At least someone understands.

I plopped down next to Rich on the couch. "It could be worse, man, my grandmother gave me musical socks one year and I had to grin and bear it, too," Rich said. I did remember those musical socks and somehow this rash-inducing sweater still seemed worse.

"Thanks man, I just can't wait for today to be over," I shrugged.

You see, I absolutely loved Christmas as a kid, but nowadays it was a drag. Right after Halloween, there's a rush to get to Christmas, and then what? New Year's and then Valentine's and Mother's Day, Fourth of July, Halloween, Thanksgiving (hardly), and we're back. Everyone thinks it's the government messing things up, but it's the holidays. Nothing can ever replace the joy felt as a child of rushing down the stairs to see what was waiting under the tree, but now it seems like everything is commercial. There's no feeling to any of it anymore. Maybe I should become Muslim.

"Well it's the best time of year, man. We did pretty well for our first semester and things are shaping up for the competition, so I think all's good," Rich reassured me. "Oh and Willoughs, I think I'm going to use one of my favors tonight that you so rightly owe me." Rich blinked as if he had an epiphany.

"Sure. What pray tell shall I do?" I replied sarcastically. Although I had a feeling I knew what it was going to be and had somehow dreaded the issue even coming up. Rich fished in his skinny jeans and pulled out what looked like a dried up piece of leaf. He placed it in my hand and grinned.

"What the heck is this?" I stared at the object in my hand.

"That, my friend, is your excuse to finally get somewhere with Alice," Rich pointed at the dried leaf.

"Is this supposed to be mistletoe? This has to be the corniest opening, Rich." I shook my head.

"Whatever works, my man," Rich replied. "You're not going to make the first move, but this will be your in. You're going to thank me later." He looked so proud of himself for thinking of this that I wanted to smack the idea off his face. At that moment, the doorbell rang, causing my heart to drop.

"I'll get it!" Ella ran over to the door.

"Willoughs, get the door, will you?" mom shouted from

the kitchen.

Rich raised his eyebrows at me as I walked to the door. I looked through the peephole to get a confirmation, and surely enough, there stood Alice with a huge dish and Chelsea by her side holding fine china as well. Who invited her? Lately, it seemed that she was warming up to Rich, but that didn't necessarily mean I wanted her to interrupt what could happen tonight. Or better yet, maybe the fact she's here could give me an excuse not to go through with it. Using this resolve, I opened the door.

"Hello ladies, welcome to my humble abode," I bowed, allowing them to come in.

"It certainly is…" Chelsea started before Alice nudged her. I could tell she was going to say something.

"Thanks so much for allowing us to share Christmas dinner with you. You have a lovely home," Alice beamed. She looked absolutely adorable. She took off her winter coat to reveal a red and silver long-sleeved dress. The skirt part was pleated and flounced right above her knees while her black ankle boots gave her a little more height than usual. Her curls were especially shiny this evening and bounced as she twirled out of the coat to hand to me. I noticed the back of her dress had a little opening on the lower back region, showing a couple swallows on her side.

Rich hopped up from the couch to tend to Chelsea and take off her coat. Her blonde hair was pulled into a sleek ponytail as she revealed a black turtleneck and long black skirt with slits on the side of it, revealing even more of her tanned and toned skin. She wore bright red lipstick, but somehow it looked better on Alice's warm natural skin than Chelsea's almost orange tone. Still, the effect from both of the girls seemed almost too grand for my frumpy sweater and what everyone else was wearing.

"I hope you don't mind Chelsea coming, but I couldn't leave her at home," Alice whispered as I took her coat.

"It's fine. I'm sure we'll have more than enough food, although it doesn't really matter in her case," I reasoned sarcastically.

Alice tapped me lightly until she noticed Ella. Ella looked up at her and Chelsea with big eyes. Alice handed me the huge dish she brought and knelt down to Ella's level.

"Now who is this cutie?" Alice said.   "Willoughs, you didn't say you had a little sister! Hi there, I'm Alice." Alice smiled her brilliant smile at Ella.

"Hi Alice, I'm Ella," Ella started uncertainly. Ella eyed Alice's curls and took in her ensemble.

"Wow, Ella, that's a beautiful name, and you have the prettiest eyes. Oh and look at your outfit!" Alice said, "Did Santa give you everything you wanted for Christmas?"

Ella nodded her head. "Yes, I got a new Barbie. Do you wanna see? Wanna play with me?"

"Sure, I'd love to," Alice smiled. "But first let me bring this dish to the kitchen and I'll be right back, okay?"

"Okay!" Ella snapped out of her trance and ran back to her dolls.

"She's so cute," Alice remarked.

"Adorable," Chelsea agreed. I hadn't even noticed her reaction, but was surprised to see her smiling after Ella.

"Willoughs, for goodness' sake, do you have any manners? Who was at the door?" my mom started as she stepped out of the kitchen, looking to see who had come in. "Oh, hello ladies. Please come on in. Oh, you didn't have to bring anything!" She came over to take the coats out of my arms to place in Rich's and motioned for him to put it in our coat closet.

"Thank you so much, Mrs. Willoughs, for allowing us to spend Christmas with you. I hope you don't mind an extra person," Chelsea replied.

"It is definitely not a problem, everyone is welcome here," my mother said. "Now you must be Alice, and who is your friend?" My mother placed her hands on Alice's shoulders and put on her most polite smile.

"Uh mom, this is actually Alice and that's her friend, Chelsea." I blushed heavily as I pointed out the correct persons. I could feel that my face was soon about to resemble my sweater.

My mother looked taken aback for a split second before regaining her composure. "Oh, excuse me. I'm sorry. Hello Alice, nice to meet you!" She shook Alice's hand feverishly, realizing her mistake.

"Hello, Mrs. Willoughs, it's fine. Most people would assume the same thing," Alice chuckled lightly. "I brought some egg salad, if you don't mind. I've been told that my egg salad is to die for! I just hope no one is allergic." Alice offered up the dish from my hand, giving my mother a sweet smile.

"Yes and I brought some apple pie, courtesy of my butler, Franco," Chelsea offered while laughing.

"Oh my, yes. Well ladies, come with me into the kitchen and I'll show you where to place them, but you really shouldn't have," my mother walked ahead of them to lead them to the kitchen. Alice smiled over her shoulder to reassure me that no foul was done as she followed them, and turned back as my mother started babbling about food.

Rich returned and placed the dried up leaf in my hand again and said, "I think that went pretty well."

"I guess," I replied with some doubt in my voice.

The doorbell rang again, startling me. Rich looked through the peephole before opening the door. "What's up, guys? Merry Christmas!"

Mike and Bill ambled inside the house with gift bags. I clapped hands with them, greeting them.

"Merry Christmas, fellas! Are the ladies here?" Mike asked. He scanned the room to check and see.

"Yeah, they went into the kitchen with my mom," I replied as I took their coats.

"Nice, nice. This should be an interesting Christmas. Both Willoughs and Rich have ladies. Bill, I think we need to step up our game," Mike and Bill moseyed their way over to plop down on the couch.

"Hey, hey, cut the trash talk out. Willoughs here has a girl. I'm just enjoying at the sidelines," Rich stated as he sat down in my father's chair adjacent to them.

"Yeah, bet you won't say that when Chelsea comes around," Bill said.

"I'm a grown man. I can say and do what I want and date whoever I please," Rich puffed his chest. I shook my head as I walked to the coat closet.

"Really, now? Hey, Chelsea!" Bill shouted.

Chelsea and I walked into the room at the same time to catch Rich punching Bill in the arm.

"Crap man! Oh, Chelsea, I just wanted to say hi. You look great tonight!" Bill rubbed his arm, looking tense.

"Thanks," Chelsea said suspiciously, looking back and forth at the two. Ella giggled in her corner, bringing the guys' attention to her.

"Ella-Bella! I didn't even see you, girl!" Mike exclaimed. He opened his arms for her to run into.

"Mike!" she laughed into his arms.

Chelsea shook her head with a smile and bent down to welcome Ella. "Ella, your mom wants you in the kitchen!"

Ella looked at her and smiled. "Okay!" Ella ran to Chelsea and held onto her skirt where the slit had almost begun. Chelsea picked her up, to Ella's delight as she loved being carried, and the two walked into the kitchen.

I walked over to the couch next to Rich and sat down heavily, sinking into its softness. Rich leaned forward to the other guys and said in a low tone, "Okay, but on a serious note, guys. Tonight's the night for our boy Willoughs and Alice."

Mike and Bill smirked to each other before I could reply. "Dude, not cool. You can't give me a dried leaf and expect me to make magic happen. It has to come naturally." The guys were all laughing hysterically when my dad walked in.

"Hey fellas, Merry Christmas! What you guys laughing about?" he placed his hands on his hips and looked at us all.

"Nothing Dad, the guys are being idiots, as usual," I muttered.

"Yeah Mr. W., don't mind us. We were just giving Willoughs here a pep talk," Mike offered with a mischievous grin.

"Mmhmm," my dad grumbled, obviously noting there was an undertone beyond his scope. "Well you boys try to behave yourselves tonight. You know how Mrs. Willoughs likes everything perfect, and as I understand, we're having even more female company, so be gentlemen."

"Yeah Dad, they're here already," I assured him.

"Well, then," dad started before mom came up behind him.

"Oh honey, glad you're here," mom kissed him on the cheek. "Alright everyone, dinner is ready if you'd make your way to the living room. Bill, Mike, glad you boys could make it!"

"Hi Mrs. Willoughs," they replied in unison. Suddenly remembering, Bill reached in his bag and pulled out a gift bag bursting with tissue paper. "Before I forget, my mother wanted me to give you this, Mrs. Willoughs. She thought you might appreciate it."

"Oh thanks, sweetie!" my mother exclaimed.

Mike pulled out a long skinny box wrapped in red paper. "My folks thought you'd like this as well, Mrs. Willoughs."

"You boys are so sweet," Mom gave them a hug and kissed them on their cheeks. "I'm so lucky to be surrounded by men who care for me, huh? Well let's go on and eat. I'll have to call your parents and thank them as well!" With her arms around them, she guided them to the dining room with my father in tow and Rich and I bringing up the rear.

Rich placed his hand on my chest to stop me and looked into my eyes with his hazel eyes that would usually get his women shaking. "Seriously, man. You have to do something tonight, we're counting on you." He patted my shoulder before spritely running up to the dinner table. I mean, what did he expect me to do?

We made our way to the dinner table where this huge feast awaited us. Ella was seated in her chair closest to mom. Alice and Chelsea were bringing out what seemed to be the last few dishes of food.

"Chelsea, I didn't know you knew how to carry dishes," I remarked in her ear as she moved to the other side of the table.

"Bite me," she glared before punching me in the arm. She put on her best smile as she made her way around the table.

Dad sat at the end of the table with mom on his left and Ella next to her. Bill sat down next to Ella, while Mike sat on my father's right. Chelsea sat down between Mike and Rich, while Alice smoothed her skirt and settled next to Rich. Thus, leaving me to sit across from Alice or at the other end of the table. Deciding across was a better course of action, I grabbed my seat next to Bill.

"Ah well, looks like everyone is here," my dad smiled. "Now, let's bow our heads to grace and take everyone's hands."

We bent our heads down and I felt a tap on my wrist from Alice. She motioned her eyebrows for me to take her hand.

"Oh, right," I muttered before taking her hand gingerly. It was still so smooth and soft from my memory. Bill knocked my leg with his knee as if to caution me. Rich smirked before my dad finally said grace over the meal. Ella was bouncing up in her seat while mom had a smile on her face. I put my head back down as my dad said the blessings for our food.

When he had finished and everyone released each other's hands, my father started again looking in the direction of our company. "So Alice Atkins, it's great for you to join us!"

Mom and everyone else had started to pass the dishes of food as Alice replied, "Thanks for allowing me into your home. You have a very lovely house." She smiled genuinely as my father raised his eyebrow for a split second as he realized which girl was actually Alice. Maybe this could have been preempted better.

"Yes, well thank you and glad you're here," my father returned a sincere smile and dished his food. "So Willoughs tells me that you all are performing together. How do you like roughhousing with these knuckleheads?"

Alice laughed and said, "Sometimes I question my decision, but the guys are sweet." She looked at the other guys who gave polite smiles before they dug into their food.

My dad scoffed at this. "Well, sweet is a nice way of putting it."

"Oh, Jim," mother tsked. "I think it's nice they have a new member, and apparently one who sounds quite lovely, at that. You know, Alice, Willoughs speaks so highly of you and your voice. You must let us hear you one day."

"I'd love that," Alice replied warmly. "I could sing something for you all after dinner, if you'd like."

"That would be lovely," my mother agreed.

"Yeah, Mrs. Willoughs, Alice is truly one of the best things for the band," Mike agreed. The other guys nodded in agreement as they stuffed their faces with food.

"Well, I'm glad," my mother said as she nodded.

Ella bounced in her seat and announced, "I like your hair, Alice. It's so bouncy!"

"Isn't it, Ella-Bella?!" I agreed, a bit too enthusiastically.

Alice's face beamed at the compliment. "Why thank you Ella, and thanks Willoughs."

I hadn't even noticed my face was cheesing so hard from the teeming compliments for Alice and I quickly turned off my smile. My father picked up on this and smirked to my mother, who also seemed to notice.

"Call me Ella-Bella, everyone else does." Ella dipped her spoon into her mouth and swallowed loudly.

"Thanks, Ella-Bella," Alice beamed. "I like that name for you."

"I like it, too," Ella took another bite as she played with her ponytail. "Do you want to meet Fairy Berry after dinner?"

Alice glanced at me before returning to Ella and said, "I would love that, Ella-Bella!"

Chelsea smiled at the exchange as everyone else smirked. They have all been acquainted with Fairy Berry. She was practically a rite of passage of acceptance to Ella's world.

I shook my head and said, "Ella-Bella, I think Alice might have some stuff to do after dinner. Maybe she can see her another time?"

"Hmph! Alice said she wants to, right, Alice?" Ella sat up in her seat to get a better assessment of any defiance that might come before mom tried to sit her down.

"It's no problem at all, I would love to," Alice reassured. "I don't have any place I absolutely have to be for a while, so it's fine." Alice gave me a questioning look. I murmured, "Well, I tried to save you."

"Willoughs, I meant to ask you, how is Lucy? You know, I haven't seen or heard from her since you moved onto campus," my mother started. Rich nearly choked on his food. Chelsea rubbed his shoulder as Alice looked at me with interest.

In fact, I have probably only seen Lucy twice since school had started, both in passing, thankfully. I felt a twinge of resent at the question, though. Why bring her up in front of Alice?

"She's fine, I guess," I shrugged. "I haven't seen her much since move-in day." I kept my face into my food avoiding my mother's and Alice's gaze. I begged fervently for the inevitable question not to be asked.

"Who's Lucy?" Alice asked.

"Oh, Lucy was a darling girl Willoughs used to date!" my mother exclaimed. "Why, she was his first girlfriend and first kiss! I have to tell you the story, you see Willoughs…"

"Mom!" I pleaded. "Could you be any more embarrassing? Can we not talk about her?"

Mom looked at me, mildly taken aback. "I just thought it was a funny story, Willoughs."

Alice looked at me surprised as well, as the other guys raised eyebrows at each other, no doubt stifling their smirks. Dad gave me a stern look, "Willoughs, that's enough."

Alice looked at me softly and stated, "Yeah, it's totally fine, Willoughs. We all have embarrassing stories, I'm sure it's not that bad. Besides, if you let my parents tell it, they can go on for hours." Alice chuckled.

"You see, Willoughs," my mother pointed out before looking over to Alice. "Oh, he gets so sensitive sometimes, but I'll have to tell you another time before he catches a hissy fit. Oh and his baby pictures! Now that'll really be embarrassing."

"I'd like to see those, too, Mrs. Willoughs," Mike chimed in. "I love that one with the cowboy hat."

"Did you ever see the one in the bathtub?" Rich edged in.

"Or the one with the sprinklers," Bill grinned.

"No, boys, you should see the one where he was trying to make a cake with his mother," my father offered.

Kill me now. I sunk my head into my hands as they offered one more embarrassing memory after another. Luckily, I had finished my food and started to get up as I could feel my pores inflame. "Well, while you all gallivant over my life's finest moments, I think I'll go get some fresh air."

"Willoughs!" my mother hissed.

"Son!" my father bellowed.

"No, it's fine, I need to take a walk. I'll be back in a few," I waved my hands as I made my way to drop my dishes in the sink.

"Hey man, we're just joshing you," Rich held up his hands in defense.

But my temples were throbbing and I could feel my whole body burning from the unwanted memories. I needed out. I felt stifled and needed to breathe. I grabbed my coat and scarf from the hallway closet amidst everyone else's winter gear and stomped outside.

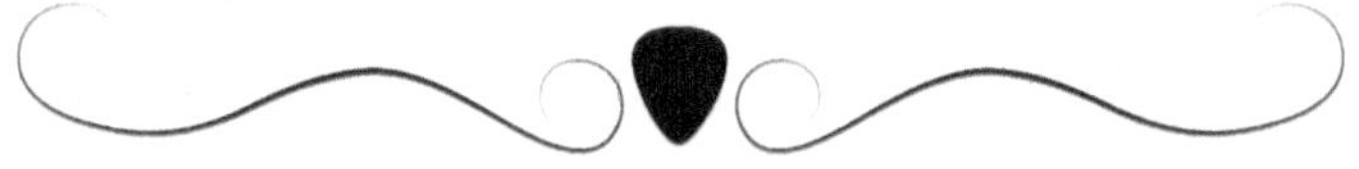

I wasn't exactly sure how long I had been walking or

where I planned on going, but I knew I needed this. My breath circled around me in faint smoke from the cold, crisp air. There was a slight wind that picked up my scarf and set it plodding down against my chest. The weatherman said it was going to snow within the next day or so, as it usually does around this time of year. I don't mind the snow so much as it's falling, but the cleaning up after I can do without. I'll probably have to lay salt later this evening.

When I went outside, I decided to make a right and walk down past Mrs. Baker's house. Nearly everyone's house down her way and across the street had lights on and cars lining the driveway. I heard a couple children giggling as they hopped out of one minivan and started racing towards Mr. Jones' house.

I remember Ella's first Christmas where it snowed and how I wanted to show her everything. She had on this teal blue jumpsuit/egg roll get-up and was the cutest thing. She waddled as she helped to make a snowman and didn't even cry when she fell down in the snow. She giggled when I threw a snowball at her and we made snow angels. It was one of my favorite snow days, if not my most favorite.

I remember we sat up watching the snow fall around our icy breaths and how one almost perfect snowflake fell right up on her nose. It was balanced there for what seemed like an eternity before Mr. Jones barked the snowflake into dissolution. Time just seemed to go by so slowly then. I told Ella and I'm not exactly sure what propelled me to say it, but I said, "Treat life just as you would that snowflake. It can appear beautiful and as stopping and waiting for us, but just like that, it can be so brief." Her ice blue eyes blinked up at me, and though she was so small, she just seemed to get me at that moment. Gosh, I loved that girl.

"Willoughs!" I heard a familiar voice yell towards me.

It sounded as if she was calling my name for a while and was exasperated. I turned around, and surely enough, Alice's mocha face and bright doe eyes were catching up with me. I hadn't even realized how far I was walking until now.

"Willoughs! Are you listening to music or something? I was calling you for a while," Alice breathed as we made our way toward each other.

"I'm sorry about that. I felt like I needed out back there. Why are you here? I figured my mother would be showing you my entire childhood," I said.

"I was worried about you, Willoughs, and besides, I think your mom and Chels are having a good time with that without me," Alice smirked. Great, I almost wished Chelsea came out for me rather than Alice. Something's telling me that I won't hear the end of this anytime soon.

"This is a really nice neighborhood, though. Walk with me and fill me in on your own childhood," Alice said as she hooked her arm into mine. I guess I hadn't realized how tall I actually was in comparison to Alice or maybe her tininess alluded me, but I felt as though I was towering above her more than usual. Maybe I grew another five inches from the BS of tonight. Who knows?

We walked forward for a bit as I tried to give my best tour guide impression. I showed her Locklear's place, who had a tire swing that all the neighborhood kids flew through at least once, and the Johnson's famously Christmas-decorated house. It was always a spectacle to see his place as it seemed that he added more lights every year. Although, he decorated for pretty much any holiday – Valentine's, Easter, Memorial Day, you name it. I remember one year, Rich dared me to take one of his decorations off for Christmas.

"Come on, Willoughs, he won't ever notice. He has so

many, it'll probably be a load off if we take a couple," Rich reasoned. I knew he would probably notice, but yet it felt like something I should do anyway. I crept up to the side of the house with my scissors and grabbed at the tangly, thorn-like wires to make my cut, but when my hand got close to the light, my hand burned! I tried for another light and another until it didn't matter whether I grabbed for the light or the wire, whatever I touched shocked and burned me.

About to throw the whole bet away, I turned to find the Johnson's dog, Rocky, snarling at me. I never ran so fast in my life. You could imagine me, red all over, smoke trailing my hands and shirt, and this Rottweiler reminding me whose domain I tried to sabotage.

Alice laughed into my arm at this story. "I remember when Mason double-dog dared me to take our dad's wallet so he could order pizza, you know, since I'm pretty small, he thought I could get away with it. Well I crawled into our parents' bedroom as quietly as I could as our dad was sleeping. He had put his wallet on the night table next to where he slept and was a pretty deep sleeper, so I thought I could get away with it, too. I remember looking up to him and seeing his eyes wide open since he sleeps with his eyes open, and when I put my hand on his wallet, he yelled so loudly I thought I would jump on the roof!" Alice giggled excessively at this memory. I found myself laughing and smiling with her. She looked so freaking adorable. Her curls were creeping from underneath her thick cap and her eyes shone so brightly.

Our breaths seemed to cloud and tangle with one another. We were at the end of the street where it changed to a wooded area past Shrive's place. The wind blew past pretty hard and pushed her curls into her eyes while also biting harshly upon my neck.

"Whoa!" we both breathed in unison and chuckled at the force. I moved to help block the wind from pushing the pixie down and she huddled into my stomach.

When the wind had lifted, I looked down at her. She had quite a few curls on her face and yet I could still see her pearly whites shining under her mass of raven curls.

"Are you okay?" I breathed. I pushed the curls from her face and tried to tuck them behind her ears. I could feel her rosy cheeks filling my hands. Her eyes were particularly bright and looked at me intently. I could feel the warmth in my hands and cheeks as I realized that I was actually touching her. I started to pull my hand away from her face, but she softly placed her hand on my wrist as if holding it there, holding this moment.

I looked to her lips, which looked sensuously full and red. I wanted no more than to kiss those lips at that instant and just enjoy that feeling of my whole lips on hers. I inched forward and had to hunch down pretty low to reach her face… so low that I lost my balance and fell on top of her!

"Ouch!" she squealed underneath me before erupting into giggles.

My face had to have been bright red. Great, when I finally have my moment, I blow it by falling on top of the girl. I rolled over and off of her, and let out a huge sigh as I closed my eyes, just ready for the day to be over with at this point.

"I'm so sorry." I started to apologize before I opened my eyes to look at her, but she was already peering down at me, her curls seeming to want to escape her hat again. Those darn curls seemed to always get to me, among other things.

She gave a small smile, pursed her lips, and bent down to give me a delicate kiss on my lips. I felt the warmth emanating from her mouth to mine, her nice full lips enveloping mine and her soft breathing from her nose. I never wanted to escape this kiss, this feeling. I placed my hand on the side of her face, my fingers playing with her curls as I kissed her deeper and deeper, enriched with her lilac scent and her nearness to me. I envisioned myself engulfed in her world full of honey, sweet warmth, strawberries, and smooth mocha wrapped in caramel and milk.

Strange how a pixie like that could stir up those feelings. But I think I'll accept it.

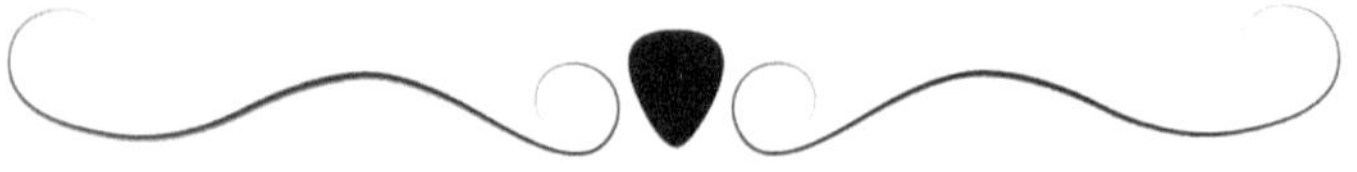

So I guess it goes without saying that Alice and I started dating after that. When we floated back to my place after that sweet make-out session, it was pretty much written all over both of our faces. The boys gave me the nod and thumbs up, my dad smirked, Chelsea rolled her eyes as usual, Ella-Bella grabbed her to play, and my mom just gave a half-smile.

After our winter recess, when we returned to campus, we were nearly inseparable. We continued practicing as usual and I went to more of her Ubuntu meetings, despite some looks from some of the members. Though I have to say I did enjoy those meetings regardless. I visited her more frequently at Sips, and when she could, she'd wait for me outside of class.

"Normally I would puke at couples like you guys, but for some reason I can't even get mad at you guys," Rich commented once. I guess he couldn't be mad because even though we were hanging out more than usual, Alice was like one of the guys anyway. She wasn't super prissy about cleanliness or our farts, burps, or truly gross debates. She would actually join us sometimes.

"Dude, you actually found a good one," Mike clapped my back. Indeed, I think I did.

After almost three months of us dating, I got what I thought would be a brilliant idea to surprise her. I ran it by the guys so I had their support at least.

This moment I remember as clear as if it were yesterday. We had finished another of our practices and Alice had to leave to spend time with her folks for the weekend.

As she slipped into the car with Mason is when it dawned on me. When they had pulled out and onto the freeway, I ran to the guys with excitement.

"Guys! Guys! I have the absolute perfect idea to surprise Alice and it'll be a great birthday gift!" I exclaimed.

Bill and Mike smirked at each other while Rich puffed at his cigarette before rolling his eyes toward me. "You know, your last idea actually worked out for you, what pray tell could be the newest of the escapades for Willoughs?" Rich asked slyly. "I think we all have an idea, though, right guys?" Rich and the guys chuckled.

"Yeah yeah, guys," I blushed. "Look I'm serious–"

"Oh, we are too!" Mike whooped. These guys are so immature.

"Look, I think I know something Alice would totally want for her birthday and then it's the competition and everything. I know she'll love it!" I enthused.

"Okay Willoughs, indulge us," Rich puffed his cigarette.

"Let's find her mom," I stated firmly. "Her biological mom."

The boys glanced at each other skeptically. "Um, Willoughs, you sure that's a good idea, man?" Rich asked hesitantly.

"Yeah, why wouldn't it be?" I asked.

"Dude, she seems pretty happy with her family and maybe there's a reason her mom isn't with her now," Bill reasoned.

"Yeah, but if you knew your mom was alive, wouldn't you be curious about where she is and how she's doing? She may be just as curious and scared to get to know her, too," I tried to reason back.

"I don't know, Willoughs, that might be heavy and didn't you say she said her mom had drug problems in the past?" Mike added.

"I know but everyone deserves to get a chance to know their mother. I just want to give that to her. You should see her. Yeah, she's happy with her family, but I know she would want to get to know her mom, too," I stated.

Rich looked at me intently as Bill and Mike looked at each other with skepticism. "Hey man, I'm willing to help, but just be careful, dude. You might open up a can of worms that doesn't need to be opened. You do realize that?"

"Look, I know her mom doesn't have the most stellar past, but there's a chance she could be feeling the exact same way Alice must be feeling," I pleaded.

Rich looked to the guys and turned back to me and broke into a grin. "Willoughs, you just might be the man. How can I help?"

I clapped his hand and patted his back. "Awesome, man. Yo, are you guys down, too?" I nodded toward Mike and

Bill.

The two exchanged another weary look until they broke into grins. "It might just be crazy enough to give a try, I'm in," Bill said.

I looked to Mike and could instantly see why he was so hesitant given what happened between him and his dad. He paused for a minute before shaking his head and clapping me on the back. "Sure, I'm in."

Our search would soon begin.

Spring.

"Willoughs? Willoughs!" a voice yelled behind me, startling me so I had to look up from my laptop.

I looked around to find Lucy standing there, holding a stack of flyers. She was wearing extremely short jean shorts showing off long slender legs, a green plain shirt open to a purple tank top, and her mousy brown hair appeared longer. Her freckles were still prominent and her skin seemed a bit browner, as if at the start of a tan. Standing there, she just seemed more self-assured than I remembered of the timid girl a few years ago. She seemed more confident.

"Y-yeah? How's it going, Lucy? Long time, no see!" I managed as I guarded my laptop.

"I'll say! I haven't even seen you since you moved in on campus! Where have you been hiding? I expected more of an entrance from you," Lucy stated as she plopped down right next to me. Why is she so chatty today?

"Uh, well I've been around. Still with the band, playing locally, getting ready for this competition coming up," I scratched my head.

"Oh, that's right, you're still with that band–Left Front Door?" Lucy asked as she tucked her hair behind her ear and scrunched up her nose. I used to love it when she did that; it made her freckles stand out more, but now something was different.

"Uh, Left Red Door, but yeah, we're still going strong and we play over at Sips sometimes," I replied. I noticed she smelled like cherry blossoms just then, and if you looked close enough, you could still see some freckles on her legs. She was wearing flip-flops that showed a lavender pedicure. Why was she so close to me?

"Cool, I definitely want to hear the band play. I missed you guys!" she enthused and smiled widely at me.

"Yeah sure, I'm sure the guys miss you, too," I sighed. Wait, no they didn't. The guys hated Lucy. Rich and Mike always thought she was weird and that something was off, even for me. Bill had said she had too many freckles.

"Really, you think so?" Lucy raised an eyebrow. "Well anywho, I have these flyers for a house party the Kappas are throwing this Saturday and just wanted to spread the word. I know you don't like parties, but maybe the guys would want to go?" She blinked and looked at me earnestly with her deep green eyes.

"Um cool, yeah, I'll let them know."

I started to take the flyer, but she held on to it as she continued, saying, "Yeah, they usually hold large parties and anyone who's anyone goes to them. So if you want your name out there, maybe you or the boys could come and get more buzz for your group." Again, she was peering at me intently. What was she looking for or expecting?

"Yeah, I guess that wouldn't be a bad idea," I replied honestly. I looked up at her and noticed Chester a few feet away talking to what looked like a professor, and we locked eyes. Lucy looked back to see what I was looking at and asked, "Is something wrong?"

Chester averted his gaze back to the professor and resumed their conversation as if he didn't miss a step. He had a bowtie on today, too, of all days. Gosh, I can't stand that guy.

I blinked and turned back to Lucy. "What? Oh yeah, everything's fine, Luce. I'll be sure to tell the guys." I was about to start up my laptop again to continue my research.

"Luce? Wow, I haven't been called that in like four years,"

Lucy smiled. "If you do decide to go with your boys, look for me, okay? We should catch up one of these days." Lucy sprang up from beside me so suddenly it nearly startled me.

"Sure," I replied. Honestly, I would say just about anything for her to leave. Why was she still here? "You look well, Luce. I'll catch you around."

I started typing until I realized she was still there. I looked up at her inquisitively. She looked a little uncertain of what to do next and I was briefly reminded of the timid, awkward Lucy before she seemed to snap out of it.

"Right, I'll let you get back to your work. See ya, Willoughs!" She gave me a slight peck on the cheek before she scampered off. I looked at her leave and watched her brown hair bounce as she walked over to where Chester was. He seemed to have seen the whole thing before shaking his head and walking on. Why was everyone so off today?

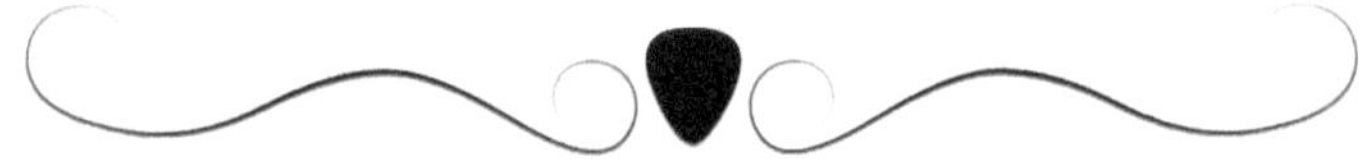

Turns out, the guys thought Lucy's idea was great, although I didn't tell them Lucy came up with it and I honestly don't know why. Why didn't I tell them Lucy invited us? Why didn't I tell Lucy I had a girlfriend? Why didn't I confront Chester sooner? I had answers for none of these because, of course, I can be a dumbass sometimes, but regardless, the guys and I decided to go to the party. Spring Break was coming up and we'd been practicing so much, outside of class and practice, I could tell this was much needed.

I invited Alice to come but it seemed as though lately she'd been spending more and more time with her folks on the weekends. I didn't want to push it too much. Her mom seemed to like me just fine, and while her dad never said otherwise, I got this feeling that he tolerated me. Not liked or disliked, per se, but tolerated. I'm not exactly sure if that's a good thing or not. Either way, the guys and I had been making gains on Alice's biological mom situation.

Rich and I narrowed down the list to about six potentials, and while I wanted to make some calls right away, Mike reasoned otherwise. "Guys, let's get out and have some fun. We have time to make calls later and I think we should really make some rounds with this party so we can actually get a following that's more than locals at Sips!"

"You're right, man. Yo Willoughs, let's just get out there and finish this weekend or something. We still have a couple weeks and I think we're making good time," Rich patted me on the back.

I blinked, moving my eyes away from the computer screen, and rubbed them while I glanced over the print-outs of several pictures and medical reports of the last ten years. I started gathering them into a red folder I kept called Alice's Project and said, "You're right, guys. Let's check this party out!"

So we got to the party, and as soon as I stepped into the yard, I wanted to go home. I could smell the weed emanating from the place and it totally looked like a frat house. It had the logo hanging on this cheap banner across the front of the house, for goodness' sake. Music was bumping so that you could hear it several houses down and there was a Slip N' Slide in the backyard with beer. Are these guys juvenile? How lame can you get?

"Guys, you know the cops are going to bust this place soon, right?" I tried to reason.

"You'd think so, but this girl in my marketing class said

that the Kappas can basically do what they want. They have loud parties and weed all the time and nobody reports them, cops don't come at all and just accept it. She said maybe because a few of their members are so rich that they just get their dads to pay them off and keep it hush-hush," Mike said.

"Hmm well that's a relief, I guess," I shrugged.

"Willoughs, live a little!" Rich tousled my hair. "Why don't you grab a beer and hang at the swing bench over there while we'll mingle? I see a little blonde right over there, but if you need us just holler, okay?" Rich eyed this cute blonde giggling with her friends. I already know how this is going to end. Ever since Alice and I have been going out, it's been on-again/off-again for Rich and Chelsea, and apparently at this moment, they were off-again. Typical.

"You know what? You guys go ahead and do that, I'll just hang here," I waved them away.

"Catch ya later, Willoughs!" the boys hollered before going up to the house.

I made my way to the swing bench Rich was referring to, making sure to step over some drunk passersby on my way there. I followed this sort of stone trail to the swing bench and laid across it as I watched over the party. Interestingly enough, I had a decent view of the party and I could only smell a faint hint of weed. I rocked back and forth using my foot on the poles and put my hands behind my head as I looked at the stars.

"KAPPAS! KAPPAS!" a huge bass voice bellowed. It almost sent me toppling over out of my daydream.

"I SAID KAPPAS!" he bellowed once more.

I looked over to where the noise was coming from. There was a large man with rippling muscles, wearing all black, standing in the middle of the backyard. His long dark dreads followed his every movement and I noticed two lines of formation gathering behind him of other guys wearing a similar get-up.

He had a hard-set jawline and dark, piercing eyes as he scoped the party. The two lines of men started marching military style passed him until he was in the direct center of their lines. Silence fell among everyone. The music was no longer playing and even the drunks had stopped laughing and gushing to witness this.

After what seemed like a strong pause, the dreaded dictator started stepping. He was stepping so precisely and choreographed, it seemed almost natural. Every move was distinct, crisp, sharp. Soon, a smaller guy moved next to him and joined in, matching his every move. Their steps were so in sync, it was mesmerizing.

The rest of the guys started murmuring underneath repeatedly, "Kappa Stone, Kappa Men, Kappa Brethren, Kappa Stone, Kappa Men, Kappa Brethren…" They increased the tempo of this gradually and the guys' steps matched their tempo so much so that it was as if the guys were floating with their steps, not even touching the ground.

"KAPPA!" the men bellowed. There was a brief pause until soon all the other men were stepping as the former two were and it seemed so fast-paced, yet in sync, that I didn't know where to look. It was as if they had so much power in their bodies, you couldn't even look away if you wanted to.

BONG! BONG!

The stepping ceased immediately.

BONG! BONG!

"KAPPA men? Who are you?" the dreaded man bellowed.

"We live by the Kappa stone which guides us Kappa men to become brethren to our own," all the men shouted in unison.

"AND WHAT DO WE LIVE BY?" the dreaded man bellowed.

"Brotherhood! Family! Respect for the stone!" the men shouted in unison.

"AND WHY ARE WE GATHERED HERE TODAY?" the dreaded man bellowed.

"We are here to show what we stand for, who we are, and to celebrate where we come from!" the men shouted.

"Well then Kappa men, I think you may have forgotten one more reason why we are here today," the dreaded man walked back and forth among the two lines of men. Each step he took was so regal and deliberate. I looked around and there was complete silence.

The dreaded man walked behind one guy who appeared to be the smallest of them all and took off his mask. He forced the guy down to his knees and beckoned for the other guy who stepped with him initially to come. I looked at this slighter guy and for some reason felt as though he seemed very familiar.

The slight guy walked over and carried a wide bowl over to the dreaded man. All other men in formation looked away towards the house and I felt my stomach begin to churn. Whatever was in that bowl was hot as you could see the steam rising from it. The dreaded man took out what appeared to be a long machete-like knife from his waist and placed it inside the hot bowl. He turned the knife over and over until he was satisfied. He brought the knife up over his head and yelled, "KAPPA!!"

I turned the other way as I could hear the knife swoop down in the air and a sizzling sound right after. I thought I heard a trace of a whimper, although I wasn't sure if it was my own or the victim's.

"KAPPA men, let us welcome our new brother!" the dreaded man bellowed. Claps from the two lines erupted, and almost hesitantly, everyone else from the party started clapping until there was full-blown applause for this guy.

The men placed a towel over the back of this guy and led him up to the house, I presume to recover. I looked to the dreaded man and he was no longer there, but the slight man who seemed his second trailed the men bringing in their new brother. He seemed oh so familiar. Could that be Chester?

"Hey Willoughs, awesome initiation, huh?" a familiar voice asked. Great.

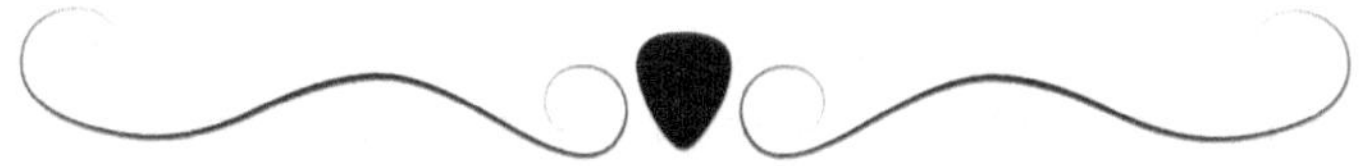

Lucy plopped herself down next to me and immediately my nostrils were hit by a deadly combination of beer and hand sanitizer. Lucy giggled to me and tossed her wavy brown hair over her freckled shoulder. She was wearing this peach colored top that seemed to complement her skin well and an extremely short metallic skirt. Her eyes seemed to be coated with a glittery pale blue as she blinked and smiled at me, although somehow the get-up didn't seem incredibly tacky. It somehow worked for her.

"Um, well if that initiation was awesome, I'd love to witness martyrdom," I retorted.

This seemed to set her off into a fit of hysteria. I feigned some laughter, but mentally kicked my own ass. That shit wasn't funny and why is Lucy acting so weird?

"Willoughs, you're so funny. You know, that's one of the things I miss about you," Lucy lingered her hand on my bicep as she held herself from the laughter. "I'm not drunk by the way, I'm just really glad you came! It feels like it's been such a long while since we hung out." Lucy looked at me earnestly and I could tell at least the latter was true.

"Yeah, it's been a while," I replied and looked toward the crowd. I couldn't force myself to lie and say I missed her, too.

"So how are you enjoying the party? Have you been here long?" Lucy inquired from a red cup. Geez, at least the Dolo cups were original.

"It's cool, I guess-," I started before Lucy interrupted.

"Hey, when is your band's next gig again? I really wanna hear you guys play! Oh and I think my voice has gotten so much better! Maybe I can be a part of your group. I have this sparkly red top that's super cute and it can go along with your group's name and..." Lucy trailed off. Honestly, when did she get so talkative? I remember when the girl was a mute!

But then it dawned on me. Shit, I really am an idiot. Just as I was about to halt this tiringly banal conversation, a sweaty light-skinned black guy approached us with similar get-up as the initiators.

"Why hello, Willoughs, glad you could make it to the party," Chester murmured. I knew that was him who was the second in command! He stood in front of us, legs apart and arms slightly bent behind him, as he peered at us bemusedly. This was sure to increase the creep factor for tonight. I swear something's off with this guy. Who stands and looks at someone like that?

"Hey, Chester man, I didn't know you were in a frat as well!" I tried to sound social and clapped Chester on the shoulder, which I immediately regretted.

Chester's bemused smile faltered slightly, but was soon replaced by a smirk as he folded his arms across his chest. "Yeah, well the tradition runs long within my family. The Marks men are Kappa men. Besides, it's another venue for me to have more social extracurriculars, which would look mighty nice for law school. But you know all about the need for social extracurriculars, don't you?" Chester clapped me back rather hard and winked. What the fuck? Could this guy be any creepier? Or corny? And I thought I was bad.

Lucy looked back and forth between Chester and I, slightly confused but definitely interested in the conversation.

"Forgive my manners," Chester extended his hand. "I'm Chester Marks IV, second in line as leader of this fine fraternity. You might have heard of my family, Marks Distributor and CO.? Finest distributor of retail?"

"Um, well I can't say that I have, but your frat gave a good show!" Lucy beamed. Ha, not everyone has heard of this stupid brand.

"Well then you haven't become as cultured as Willoughs, I see," Chester remarked with a smug grin. "Fitting."

"Dude, I don't know what your problem is but I think it's high time you leave us alone," Lucy stood up defiantly to the Carlton wannabe. Double ha.

"Hmm," Chester looked at her with contempt. "Enjoy the party, you two." Chester bowed and started to walk away when he decided to glance back and add, "Oh and Willoughs, can you tell Alice I have the kente material at my place whenever she's ready to pick it up? As a matter of fact, I think I'll text her myself and let her know I ran into you." Chester threw up a smirk in our direction before disappearing into the partygoers.

"What was that all about?" Lucy asked after a pause. "Please don't tell me you and him are friends, because he seems super arrogant. And who's Alice?"

I turned to her and started to answer just as Rich came from out of nowhere and giggled into my shoulder, tousling my hair. "Yo, this party is wild!" He laughed heavily into my shirt until he saw Lucy and finally gained his composure. "Whoa! Lucy Loose-say!! How have you been?" Rich grunted, almost sobering himself before looking at her blandly.

"Richie Rich, not much has changed, huh?" Lucy raised an eyebrow.

"I could totally say the same about you," Rich pointed, before it seemed as though he would lose his balance. I grunted under his weight. "C'mon dude, what were you doing?"

"Aha, wouldn't you like to know?" Rich nodded and pointed hard towards my chest. I thought this was my chance to leave.

"Okay man, let's get out of here. You're smoked," I tried to reason and lift him up. Lucy immediately came to help carry the sorry bastard on my other side as she let Rich rest his other arm across her shoulder. "Lucy, you don't have to help…"

"Please, Rich is nothing. I've fared worse," Lucy smiled up to me in an almost peculiar way.

"Willoughs man, I really don't feel good or comfortable in this position. Maybe you could carry me out without weighing down the poor girl," Rich tried to urge under his sweat mop of hair.

"Shut up, Rich!" Lucy snapped. "Now let's get you to your car."

Rich looked up to me with an uh-oh sort of look as we hobbled toward the front of the house and toward our car. I remember seeing Chester looking at us, still smirking as we made our way to the car, and for some reason, my chest was starting to feel heavy, with what I wasn't quite sure.

When we had finally made it to the car and plopped Rich inside, I immediately took out my cell to text Mike and Bill.

RICH IS GONE, LET'S GET PIZZA. I texted Mike and Bill and slid my cell into my back pocket. That was usually code for let's get the fuck home, although we haven't really used it in a while.

After Lucy had settled Rich, she came to the front of the car next to me and said, "I'm sorry you have to leave so soon. I wanted to spend more time with you." Lucy gave a half-smile. Ugh, I hate awkward situations like these.

"Uh Lucy? I should probably tell you something…" I started before she cut me off again.

"You have a girlfriend. Alice, right?" Lucy continued her half-smile and threw her wavy hair over her freckled shoulder.

"Uh..Yes! Yes! So…" I started again before she placed her fingers to my lips.

"Don't worry, Willoughs, I figured there was someone else and when that Chestnut guy acted weird, it pretty much confirmed it," Alice reassured. I breathed a sigh of relief into her fingers. She was making this easier than I thought it would be.

"Although," Lucy gave a coy smile and slowly brought her fingers down from my lips. "I will say Alice is extremely lucky to have you." I felt my cheeks blush a thousand degrees and knew my face must have been a tomato at this point. Why was she suddenly so close to me?

Lucy gazed up at me beneath what seemed like infinitely long brown eyelashes, and before I could object, she kissed me squarely on the mouth. Her mouth felt extremely warm on my already warm face, even after her surprisingly cool fingers found the sides of my face. I felt her tongue searching to open the crevice of my mouth before I came out of my shock and a huge buildup rising in my chest.

HONK! HONK! H-hh-h-hh-HONK!!!!

The car horn startled both of us and I immediately felt the urge to hurl. I caught a glimpse of Rich's shocked face before I saw Mike and Bill ambling along towards the car.

"What the fuck, Rich??" Lucy shrieked. Then, without fully meaning to, or perhaps part of my subconscious meant to, I hurled my guts onto Lucy's bare freckled feet. I hope Alice doesn't kill me.

So Alice didn't end up killing me, although it was clear that she was hurt. Naturally. I mean that was a fucked up thing to do and I should have realized sooner. Though I do give myself props that I told her before Chester had a chance to. On the other hand, I still feel crappy, so I'm really banking on this reunion with her mom at our concert.

Luckily, Alice still agreed to do that. And for all intents and purposes, she's still my girlfriend, albeit a limited one as she wanted just a bit of "space." And by space I mean just practice, our Ubuntu meetings, and an occasional text. I really think, though, that this performance will do us both good. We only have a few days left, and while I am anxious about this performance, part of me, or I should say the majority of me, is nervous about the reunion. I will admit that I found some interesting stuff on Alice's mom.

Mike and Bill had eventually fell off the project as there were midterms and such to worry about, amongst other things, so Rich and I picked up the slack, which was fine. The less people who knew about Alice's mom's past, or shall I say Patricia's past, the better. Drugs, an abusive guy, moving to different states— yeah, that's all in Patricia's file. As we were getting close to the actual concert, part of me wanted to call it all off, but yet some part of me felt that I should keep going, you know?

I tried to get information from Alice's folks, but it's been pretty hush-hush with them. My efforts were slightly diminished after the Lucy incident, but the scraps I could get here and there were slightly helpful. I got from Alice's mom that they were close friends in high school and college. I got from Alice the pictures and her own admission that her biological mom wasn't going through a good time when she was born. Heck, I even got from Mason that he'd seen her once or twice when he was really little (hard as that might be to imagine) and that she'd seemed "nice" and "sweet."

Indeed, when I finally reached out to her, she did seem genuine that she wanted to see Alice. Mind you, Rich and I were the ones conducting the research, and after finally scouring for a college yearbook and deducing from a handful of women who could've been Alice's mom, we found the one and verified through Google.

I remember the heavy skepticism Alice's dad gave me

every time I so much as mentioned Alice's mom or asked about her. Though with all due respect, it's none of his business. Alice has the right to know, right? Anyone who tries to impede that is just as wrong as the person who had to step out, and from my research it seemed as though Patricia had a rough time and needed an out.

Gosh, I hope Alice could forgive me through this. It could literally be the best thing I've done for this relationship, or the worst.

Since the Lucy incident, I did tell Lucy what she did wasn't cool and that she had to respect my relationship, and I formally cut all ties with her. I told Alice as much and the boys even backed me up, though they never cared for her much, anyway.

"Dude, how could you just let her kiss you?" Mike asked, disgusted as I'm sure all the guys felt on the inside, including me. I think my upchucking on her feet gave her a clue, though, and she's since stopped seeking me out.

Although, even with all those measures, I know Alice is hurt. It's probably not even hurt but more so disappointment as she knew I wouldn't intentionally do something like that to her. At least I hope she did.

"Willoughs, what are you thinking about in that big ol' head of yours?" Alice finally inquired, breaking up my reverie. She looked at me speculatively from her book by Ta-Nehisi Coates. Good works from that one.

"I'm just thinking over this surprise I have planned for your birthday," I half-smiled as I went back to reading my physics textbook.

"Willoughs, don't do that," Alice moaned. "You can't say that you're surprising me."

"Okay, I won't say it," I resolved.

Alice smirked at me and shook her curly-haired head. The sun glossed over her hair and made it look almost brown in its radiance. It suited her cocoa skin immensely and her smirk brought out the cutest dimple. Alice returned to her book. Oh yeah, maybe this surprise won't be so bad after all.

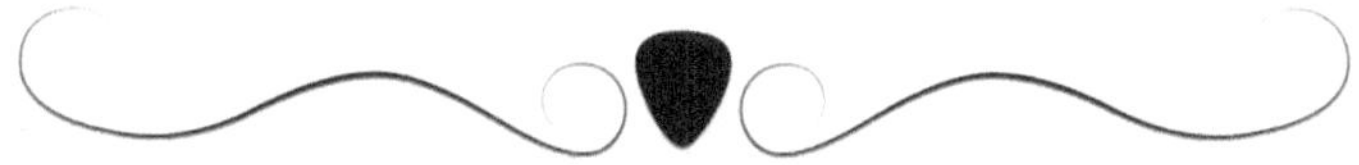

So, I'll start by saying this was probably the worst day of my life.

Nothing was going right. Mike wasn't feeling well. Bill was stuck in traffic because the dumbass decided to visit his uncle who lives like two cities away. One of the guitar strings broke even though it was a new one. Rich wasn't in a good mood, yet again, because just as Chelsea seemed to want to give them another chance, some chick said that he fucked her the night before. Even Alice was on edge, but it seemed to be more than just pre-show jitters.

"What is going on? What's going on? This day is supposed to be a great one!" I scratched my head and kicked the wall.

"Not everything can be perfect, Willoughs, just relax," Alice snapped back to me before biting her nails. Wait, she never bites her nails.

I looked around and saw other groups checking their sound qualities, some talking to tech and stage guys, some walking back and forth, some praying. Rich was huddled in the corner, one hand covering his ear as he was probably dialing Chelsea or Bill for the hundredth time. Mike was sitting on one of the amplifiers, sweating profusely and gulping down water to keep the green in his face at bay.

The first two acts that had performed sounded great and there were still about five or six groups ahead of us waiting for their turn. Perhaps today wasn't the best day to have Alice meet her mom. I triple checked outside of the curtain and there she was sitting in the center of the fourth row. Alice definitely resembled her mom – same mocha skin, dimpled cheeks, bright eyes. Her mother was slightly thinner, if that could be possible, and she looked tired, but she was definitely Alice's mom, no question about it.

"Willoughs, maybe you're psyching yourself out by constantly looking out there. Just stand with me, please?" Alice reached out her hand. I took it automatically and enveloped her into a deep hug that seemed to almost soothe us both.

"I'm sorry if I'm a bit on edge. My dad was acting super weird and my mom was like tight-lipped about something. I know something's up and it just bothers me because we always tell each other stuff, but we're going to be okay today, you hear me, Willoughs?" Alice looked up to me earnestly.

I sighed and gave a half smile. "I hope so."

"I know so," Alice resolved, and with that turned on her little pixie heel. She opened up her gig bag and pulled out what looked like a small white pill bottle. She headed over to Mike and helped to lay him down and popped a couple tablets from the bottle into his mouth, made him drink huge gulps of his water, and took off her leather jacket to cushion and prop his head.

Then she took out her cell phone and walked towards Rich's direction. "Chelsea? It's Alice, can you come backstage and help me with my makeup please? This glittery one is getting all over the place…Thanks girl!"

Alice made a second call. "Bill, what route are you on? Okay, I figured. Why don't you just take exit 3? We probably won't be on for another two hours and that way you'll be here in like forty minutes…Okay? Great! See you soon, man!" Alice hung up and turned around just in time as Chester came ambling towards her.

"Hey Alice, I brought like the whole pack of strings since I wasn't sure how much you needed. Plus, I wasn't sure how prepared you guys were and brought a tuner, a capo, cleanser…" Chester swung over his bag to show her his digs. Lately, it seemed as though the two had gotten closer, but after what I had done with Lucy, I didn't think it was my place to say anything. I still couldn't stand him, though.

"Dude, we just needed a couple strings…" I started before Alice cut me off abruptly.

"Willoughs!" Alice glared me down and turned into a bright smile at something beyond me. "Chester, thanks so much for bringing it! Willoughs, can you show Chester how to restring these guitars? Rich, Chelsea – we need to talk." Before either Chester or I could object, Alice already roped her arms into Rich and Chelsea's arms and walked them some ways ahead.

"She really is something, eh, Willoughs?" Chester threw a half-smile. He took out a string and began restringing Bill's guitar. He did this deliberately and slowly, making sure he was tightening it just right. "This guitar is beautiful. My folks made me play the violin when I was younger, but I always wanted to play the guitar. And perhaps a sax." Chester looked up to me half-expectantly and curiously, as if trying to figure me out.

I sat across from him and began restringing my own guitar, "Yeah, well guitar was always it for me. I tried the piano briefly but guitar was really my thing. I can see you playing the sax, though."

"Really? I begged my parents to let me learn when I was younger but they didn't see that for me. They wanted something a bit more classical. More in line with their vision for me," Chester sighed.

I looked over to him as he twirled his finger over the finished string and inspect the guitar further. Bill could've actually used a new guitar, but had been saving up for this really high-end one. Almost as if noting the condition of the guitar, Chester unhooked a couple of the other strings and started to slowly and deliberately restring those as well.

"Well maybe you could start it up now. Take a lesson here or there of the sax. I mean, you have an allowance or something so I'm sure it won't be that steep for you," I reasoned. "And hey, if ever you get a guitar, I could give you some pointers." Why I offered, I'm not entirely sure, but I was starting to get the feeling that Chester didn't have too many friends.

Chester blinked back up to me and gave a hint of another half-smile. "You don't think I would've thought of that by now, Willoughs? But thanks for the offer." Chester scoffed and I immediately regretted even offering the prick an ounce of my time and talent.

"Just stating the obvious, I guess," I shrugged as I was still working the string on my guitar.

Chester glanced at me as he made his way to the third string. "Look man, I'm sorry. I get that you don't like me that much."

"Hmph," I wholeheartedly agreed.

"I just really care about Alice," he went on. "She's like

one of my best friends, almost a sister to me, you know? And I don't like seeing her hurt." He reached out to grab my arm and looked at me in earnest. "I know you're not a bad guy, Willoughs, and quite honestly, I wasn't even going to tell on you of what had happened."

Now it was my turn to scoff until he squeezed my arm. "I'm serious. If anything, I was probably going to give you shit about it until you eventually told her. But you know what? I really respect that you told her as soon as you did. I don't think most guys would do that. I'm not even sure if I would, to be honest, but you definitely earned some respect in my book." Chester patted my arm and then returned to finishing the last string.

Hmph, like I needed his respect. I nodded and turned to my string. Well, maybe he wasn't so bad after all. "Yeah, I would never hurt Alice. Not intentionally anyway. I love her, man."

I paused as I finally finished tying up the string. I had never said that aloud before. I was certainly thinking it for some time and felt it for quite a while. At first, I thought it was gas or some imminent heartburn, but I soon realized I did care for her that much. I never felt like this for anyone else. I hadn't even told Rich, and with that, I turned to look at whatever miracle Alice had sprung.

When I turned, Rich and Chelsea had gathered in this full embrace as Rich was kissing the side of Chelsea's hair furiously and holding her like he never wanted to let her go. Maybe Rich won't admit it any time soon, but I could tell at that moment that he actually did care about Chelsea more than he was letting on and wanted to admit to himself.

Alice stepped back from what appeared to be a back-again couple, arms crossed as if she'd done her duty, and started making her way towards Mike, who was looking a little better.

Chester raised an eyebrow. "Well, love or not. I'll still kick your ass if you decide to hurt her again, Willoughs, I swear to-"

"Hey Chester, let me ask you something," I interrupted.

"Uh, okay?" Chester blinked.

"Why haven't you and Alice ever...you know? Hooked up or anything? Besides you being her "brother" and all because I really don't buy that. You can't just be friends with Alice," I reasoned.

Chester blinked hard and placed the newly strung guitar back in its case. He stood up and dipped his hands into the front pockets of skinny jeans that probably no man should ever try to wear. "You're right, Willoughs. I do love her and would do anything for her, but she doesn't love me." Chester swallowed hard as if he had almost come to terms with that last part as well until he added, "If she ever comes to her senses and wants me, I'm here for her. Though I'm good with being her friend until she decides otherwise."

A part of me found it unsettling for him to have those other motives, and yet at the same time, I really couldn't blame him. It's hard not to love her.

We both looked at her as she checked up on Mike and wiped at his brow with a paper towel. Mike was talking animatedly and was even gulping down some grapes and cookies that the stage people had set for the performers. Alice nodded and smiled appropriately at all he was saying, and even across from the other performers checking their equipment and the bustle of people running back and forth, I could still discern her laugh. It was rich and melodious even amongst the bustle.

Alice looked towards us and was taken aback at first that we were both looking over at her at the same time, until she broke out into a huge grin with her dimples full force. Alice waved and wiggled her fingers at us.

I could feel us both smile at her recognition of us. "Everything good over there, guys?" she called out to us. I gave her the thumbs up as Chester nodded in affirmation. Alice giggled and returned to her conversation with Mike.

"Hey guys, I finally made it! So so sorry, traffic was so backed up. I totally didn't even realize that exit until Alice told me about it," Bill clapped me on the back and nodded to Chester. "Well looks like my guitar is in good shape!" He picked up his guitar quickly and admired the new strings.

"Yeah, it took me a little bit, hope it plays fine," Chester replied modestly.

Bill twanged his fingers over the guitar, and though the notes were a bit sharper as they were new strings, it did sound fresher and cleaner. "Thanks, man. I'm going to have to change the other strings, but since I see you have the whole caboodle right here, she'll be playing fierce in no time! Bill, by the way, who are you?" he asked as he extended his hand towards Chester.

"My bad. Chester, my man." Chester shook his hand back. "I'm a friend of Alice's, but hey, you guys have a good gig. I think I should make my way to a seat since it's getting a bit packed in here."

Indeed it was as these other performers were coming off the stage and starting to really crowd the area backstage.

"Thanks man, see ya!" Bill called out as Chester disappeared out the back.

"Left Red Door? Left Red Door?" a pimply, bespectacled and really curly-haired guy shouted.

"That's us!" Rich clamored towards us, arm around Chelsea. You could see both of them were slightly flushed and bright red. Even Chelsea underneath her almost-orange-tan.

"Left Red Door, you have about two groups ahead of you now. I'd say in the next hour, you'll be up," pimply face assured.

"Cool man, got it. Thanks!" Rich replied before turning to us. "Bill, you made it! Awesome! The whole gang is here and looking back together. Even Mike! Yo, Willoughs, that Alice is a Godsend!" Rich clapped me on the back before he went back to making out with Chelsea.

"I know she is, man," I glanced over to her.

It was finally our turn. This was it.

"Left Red Door!!" the announcer roared into the microphone.

Rich slapped me on the back before making his way onto the stage as Bill and Mike shuffled up their equipment. Alice squeezed my hand tight before throwing on a show face and stepping out, waving to the crowd and shining her brightest smile. I shuffled my feet behind them and looked out to the crowd.

My mom was clapping furiously from the center of the sixth row. Dad was clapping Ella-Bella's hands with his own right next to her. Rich's mom was in front of my folks and Bill's mom wasn't too far off. I could see Alice's parents on the left side of the stage, but proud and screaming for her nonetheless, and Chelsea and Mason were beaming right alongside them. I turned to find Alice's biological mom on almost the complete right of the room and noticed as her face gave a slight recognition before her eyes started to look glossy and she gave a small smile. Gosh, Alice looked so much like her, it wasn't even funny. I shook my head and allowed the bright lights to bore into my eyes and forehead, almost blinding and burning me with its rays.

"Are you guys ready for Left Red Door!!" Rich yelled into the microphone as the audience applauded even more.

"I don't think I can hear you! Are you guys ready?" Alice backed him up with even more exuberance and the audience yelped and clapped even louder. On that note, Mike clicked his drumsticks as Alice and Rich bobbed their heads waiting for their mark.

Bill struck a chord and I soon followed suit. We were starting with one of my own personal favorites, "Tree Rock," but yet something was a little off. I chanced a look over to Mike but he was fine and the rhythm was intact on his end, and then I realized Bill's guitar gave a slight twang, probably because of all the new strings. Yet, even though it was off, it still fit the song in a weird way.

Alice brought the mic to her lips and sung in her warm, rich voice as clear as day.

"When I look back upon my life I find I cannot forget you /Cannot forget you..." She closed her eyes and let her voice take over. The crowd seemed to eat it up and was just as mesmerized by her as I usually find myself, so that the slight twang in Bill's guitar didn't even matter anymore.

When the song got to the chorus, Alice and Rich faced each other and their chemistry just worked.

They sang, "Why can't we return together? /Together? Together again? Together again? /Why can't we return together?/Why can't we?"

I found myself getting goosebumps as Rich's raspy voice mellowed and reverberated off of Alice's own warm voice. Perhaps the difference in their singing styles is what complemented the song so well, and that was the experience itself. I could tell the effect it was having on the audience, and as it was a slower song, their appreciative nods and transfixed eyes on the two front in center was reassuring to me.

I found myself glancing back and forth between Alice's dad and her biological mom for some reason, yet both seemed equally proud of Alice. After a while, though, my fingers just picked and strummed as naturally and rhythmically as Alice and Rich's voice allowed me.

We finished the first set, and went on to the second and the third. The audience was feeling it and our last set was supposed to be a quick, up-tempo song to round out our set. As Alice stepped up to the mic, I heard the slightest bit of a falter in her register. Mike covered it up quickly with the drums so it was barely noticeable, but I picked up on it.

Alice started again. Better, but not quite the best she's practiced. I glanced over to her quickly and noticed her eyes focused on the corner of the room where her mother sat. I could sense the slight look of confusion on her face as she tried to quell with keeping face for our set.

Rich took center stage, taking over her beginning solo, which seemed to rouse her out of her semi-trance. She glanced at me with her wide doe eyes almost in shock. I gave her a quick nod of reassurance, my eyes pleading her to go on and continue what we started. She shook her head slightly and then marched forward on the stage confidently and picked up Rich's part just like a pro.

When I turned back to the crowd, there didn't seem to be any notice over what just transpired, but rather just heavy appreciation. Alice's mother looked at me with a slight look of worry, but then quickly gave a half-smile. I guess so that she wouldn't derail me as well.

Taking that note, I turned back to my guitar and counted my cues. My solo riffing was at the end of the song and the part I always looked forward to.

If we could just get through this song okay, we'll deal with whatever later, I tried to tell myself over and over again. Just get through the song, get through the solo, get through with life, get through the song, through the solo, through with life....

I felt my head start to spin and my eyes were becoming foggy. Now is NOT the time, c'mon Willoughs!

I felt a little misstep in my strumming of my guitar. I tried again, and it was better, but my head was really starting to reel. If I could pull myself together for literally one more minute, we would be home free.

I decided to focus exclusively on the cues and find an anchor. Rich and Alice were really vibing off of each other, and Bill and Mike were in sync. Nearly everyone in the crowd was getting up on their feet, screaming and whistling their delight.

"YEAH, WILL-OOHS!!" I managed to hear Ella's voice among the cheering. "GO WILL-OOHS!!"

I jerked my head to her direction and noticed she was sitting on my dad's shoulders as he rooted and bobbed his head to our music. I couldn't help but feel warm inside from the sight. Screw me for having the best little sister any guy could ask for.

With that, I had to push through and keep my anxiety in check, if only for Ella. In two cues, then one cue, it was my turn.

Alice and Rich started to separate to allow me to do my solo and riff. I felt the boost of static in my fingers and picked and strummed my guitar like there was no tomorrow. The light fell dead center on me and with each stroke and pick, I felt as though my fears dissipated one by one until I was just left with myself and my guitar. Nothing else mattered at that moment but my vibes and the crowd's reaction to my energy.

When I struck my last chord, I even extended it so much that the crowd went really fucking wild. My fingers throbbed from the pulsating heat and my hands felt warm and tingly. I exhaled and absorbed the crowd's thunder, and when I thought I had enough, Alice and Rich came to my sides and put their arms around me. Alice pulled my head down quickly for a kiss and her lips almost sent me reeling again. When she was about to pull away, I held onto her for a few seconds longer and could feel approval from the crowd. I might as well try for as many good moments now as I can, right?

"Willoughs, you were freaking awesome!" Alice finally managed to squeal after our kiss.

"You're fucking awesome, I love you, Alice!" I yelled amongst the bustling of the massive standing ovation.

Alice gave a half-smile and said, "I love you too, Willoughs."

We gushed at each other before I pulled her into a bear hug. She and I waved back to the crowd and made our way off-stage as the announcer waited for the crowd to simmer down.

"Willoughs man, I've never seen you kill the end like you just did!" Rich exclaimed.

"Yo dude, that was wicked! I think we did really well. Look at that crowd!" Mike enthused.

Bill patted me on the back and said, "Great job, guys. I think that was literally our best!"

"I'm so proud of us!" Alice agreed. "Gah, c'mon, group hug!"

We all huddled up and we were soon joined by Chelsea and Mason.

"You guys were so good. I think you might just win this thing!" Chelsea praised before Rich swept her up into his arms to spin her around in their excitement.

"Great job, little sis, you were so badass out there!" Mason remarked as he gave her a huge hug.

"Thanks so much, Mason!" Alice gushed. "That means a lot!"

"Guys, I don't know about you, but I'm freaking famished after that. I'm gonna go chill near the snack table if anyone wants to come," Bill offered.

"Yeah me too, I'm coming," Mike sighed.

"And me, I'll catch you in a few, sis," Mason said over his shoulder.

"Mmph, wait for us," Chelsea added as she let go of Rich.

As our group moseyed over to the snack table, which somehow seemed more replenished than before, Alice glanced up to me and asked, "Wanna grab something, Willoughs?"

"I think I just want to catch my breath for a few right now," I replied and suddenly felt the need to sit. "Are you okay, though, Alice?"

"I'm great, my mind is just reeling! It was so great to be on stage with that crowd, I'm just…whew!" she breathed as we both took a seat. "Although, I will say that during like our third song, I saw a lady in the crowd who looked awfully familiar and that bugged me out for a good couple of minutes." Alice's brow furrowed.

"Yeah, I kinda noticed. Um.." I began.

"You noticed too, huh? I mean, luckily, Rich snapped me out of it, but it seemed to work, right? Thank God the audience didn't pick up on that!" Alice proclaimed.

"Yeah Alice, listen, I…" I started again.

"Man, you guys are the best. If someone didn't snap me out of it, I don't know what. I mean, this might sound crazy, but that woman almost looked like my mo - " Alice continued until she saw the same woman walking toward us from the side door.

Alice's mother walked steadily toward us and appeared to be holding a bouquet of yellow roses and a soft smile on her warm brown face. "Alice? Sweetie?" The woman walked over, almost hesitant.

Alice looked at her, confused and in shock.

"Alice, I've been trying to explain but…" I began again.

Alice whipped her head back to me. "This isn't what I think it is, is it, Willoughs?"

I could hardly read her face at this moment. I couldn't tell if she was angry, pissed, hopeful, confused, or perhaps she was all of this and more. Maybe shock is the perfect summation of how she was feeling.

"Patricia, what the fuck are you doing here?!" Alice's dad bellowed.

"Marcus!" Alice's other mom squealed.

"Don't Marcus me! This woman has done nothing but cause pain in our lives and now she turns up out of the blue on this night of all nights!" Alice's dad yelled. He looked positively seething. His face was turning bright red and his fists were heavily clenched at his sides. I had never seen him this upset, even at me.

"Marcus, Claire, I don't mean any harm," Patricia started. "I just wanted to see my daughter, and when Willoughs said it would be fine that I attended…"

"Willoughs!" Councilman belted and looked at me menacingly. "You're going to take advice from a child to come here instead of speaking to us first? The ones who've raised your daughter? With no support from you at all, mind you?"

"Sir, with all due respect, Alice has a right to know her mother and I thought…" I tried to reason.

"Willoughs, pipe it! I decide what is right for my daughter. That is not of your concern, nor is it your call," Councilman stated. "My God, Alice, where did you find this guy? You would've done better with Chester. Alice, get your things. We're leaving and I don't want you to have anything else to do with this woman or Willoughs."

"Okay dad." Alice complied with a sullen look on her face.

"Alice? Sir? Alice?" I looked from side to side, hardly believing what was happening. "You can't be serious? Alice?"

"Willoughs, really and truly, it wasn't your call and you

should've at least told me before you decided to do this." Alice went to gather her bag, not even looking me in the eye.

I turned to look from Alice's biological mother and Mrs. Atkins, both of who seemed resolved about Councilman's decision.

"Willoughs, it's fine. It's not the right time," Alice's biological mother reasoned with a sheepish smile.

"Nor will it ever be the right time," Councilman interjected.

"Marcus, enough!" Mrs. Atkins hissed before turning to me. "Willoughs, I know you mean well but there are some affairs you just don't dive into without knowing the whole story."

"Mean well? The boy wasn't thinking at all!" Councilman bellowed. "If you so much as step a foot in my house ever again or think of calling Alice…!"

"Hey! What's going on here?" Rich shouted. A crowd of people was starting to come observe the commotion we were apparently starting. My parents and Ella were making their way through the crowd.

"It's none of your concern, boy!" Councilman stated as Alice finally hurried back with her bags and gear in tow.

"Boy? What kind of way is that to talk to anyone?" my dad started.

"Excuse me?" the Councilman started to get riled up again.

"Dad, let's go! I'm sorry, everyone, for the commotion," Alice said as she tried to calm everyone.

"Marcus, let's go," Mrs. Atkins tried to grab ahold of her

husband.

"You heard me damn right, and I don't care if you're Councilman or not!" my dad started again.

Oh no, when my dad starts to get upset, you have to watch out. Suddenly, my mind was getting foggy again and I was becoming dizzy looking at this spectacle. My after-show buzz was faltering as it looked like Alice's dad was sure enough about to clock mine.

"Stop guys, stop!" I tried to yell but it felt hollow. As if I hadn't yelled at all. It almost felt as though I was rising above this squabble and watching down on the fight between the two men, and the crowd seemed to be getting larger to watch the fight.

My mother and Alice's mother were both screaming and begging their husbands not to fight while the band was trying to push everyone else away.

Ella covered her ears and screamed at the top of her lungs until more stage hands and security could come to see what was happening. I wanted to do more since this was my fault, but I felt my body drift further and further away. Until it was all black.

145

Summer (Again).

I grabbed another box from the delivery truck to restock in the back of the store. I opened the box and pulled and priced college sweatshirt after college sweatshirt. Ross was about to clock out for the day and Jan was still checking and counting the register.

For all intents and purposes, the campus was basically closed for the summer, and in a way I kinda preferred it that way. I mean, of course, there were still summer classes and all but the campus was calmer…peaceful…quiet. After all that happened after the spring concert, I needed this reprieve.

My folks asked about me coming home for summer break, and even though I missed being at home, I really needed to stay here.

"Why stay at the school, man? You know you're free to chill at my place," Rich reasoned when I mentioned I was staying.

"I know but I need the extra cash and plus I might take up a class or two. I'm gonna need it after Calculus IV," I tried to counter. Bullshit. Like I'd ever take up another class willingly, especially for Calculus IV.

"Hmm, okay man." Rich could see through my bull but knew not pester me further. "Look, you better still make it to practice on time this summer. We need to get started on a CD soon."

"Yeah, yeah, I'll be there," I scratched my head.

"I'm serious, Willoughs. I'm here for you, man," Rich added with a note of sincerity as he placed his hand on my shoulder and looked me in the eyes.

"I know, man." I was trying to avoid his gaze. I knew what he was referring to and it was still a soft spot for me. Needless to say, Alice and I were through, and I felt devastated so there was no need to rehash those feelings. Rich threw me one more sympathetic look before running off to finish packing his stuff to leave. Mike and Bill were going to travel with Bill's folks to Florida for a couple weeks and we were supposed to meet up to rehearse once they got back, so that left my friend ratio to zero for the summer.

I decided to plug in my headphones as I priced the rest of the sweaters. Ross tapped me on the shoulder, wished everyone a good summer and left, leaving just Jan and I to tend the store. I blasted up "Bittersweet Symphony" as I priced the remaining sweaters. How fitting.

"Willoughs! Willoughs!" Jan yelled over my headphones.

I lowered the volume thirty decibels before turning over to her direction.

"Dude, you don't have to stay here. I'll take care of the rest of those," Jan blinked at me. Now she had pink and purple hair and looked more anime than ever.

"It's fine, Jan. I need the extra dough," I sighed as I started to turn back to my music and boxy college sweaters.

"Willoughs, what's wrong with you, man?" Jan asked. "Ever since that concert, you haven't been the same old sarcastic Willoughs. You've grown dour and it's so not your vibe. I know not winning couldn't have bummed you out that much." Jan's eyes grew weary even stating this obvious fact. Although in truth, even though we didn't win first at the concert, we did get second, and by all accounts would have won first if the after show brawl hadn't occurred, but that's a whole other issue.

"Nothing, Jan. I'm just getting a bit more serious about my future in retail is all," I replied and threw a half-smile and a price sticker for flare.

"I'm serious, Willoughs," Jan yawned. "I mean, I do appreciate the increased work effort and productivity, but I'm really interested in the reason behind this change."

"Jan, just drop it. I'm fine. Be glad my ethic improved at all, despite everything," I sighed again and put my headphones in. I could feel her gazing at me for a few moments longer before shrugging my melodrama off and returning back to her receipts.

My mom texted me, asking me to watch over Ella this upcoming weekend since she and dad were going away on a conference for his job.

Sure, I texted back. When I clicked out of the message, I couldn't help but notice the last few times I texted Alice with no reply.

I love you, I'm sorry.

Can we talk?

I understand it was not my call nor right to contact your mom without telling you or your folks and I'm soooo sorry. Please can we talk?

I love you, I'm sorry.

I love you..

I'm sorry…

So pitiful, right? I tried calling her house too, to at least try to have a civil conversation with her dad, but to no avail. That guy would not budge. I even apologized to Alice's biological mom, perhaps the only one receptive to me right about now, but I guess she's used to their cold shoulder at this point.

I contemplated leaving another text message, but decided

against it. I put the phone back in my pocket and bit down on my lip hard as I felt my face redden. I had half a mind to just delete all of those dumb text messages and be done with it. They act as though I committed murder or something. I shook my head.

As I priced the last sweater from the box, Jan called out to me again. "Um, Willoughs?"

"Geez, what is it, Jan? What?" I turned around exasperated, headphones popping out of my ears, and then immediately halted. I drew in a breath at the sight of the Councilman, standing there austerely as if without a care in the world. His crisp dark suit and green tie were immaculate, and yet watching him stand there in a college bookstore seemed almost out of place, yet not at the same time.

"Why, hello Willoughs," Councilman started out slowly and evenly.

"H-hello, Councilman," I gulped. I sort of remembered the last time we had seen each other, which wasn't all too pretty, and I was knocked out for the brunt of it.

Jan stared back and forth between us, interested, yet slightly scared of what might transpire between us. Though truthfully, Alice's dad was a pretty big and intimidating guy. When I had woken from my blackout, I was a bit surprised that both my dad and Alice's got good licks in. Some would say my dad won and others said that Alice's dad held a decent number against my old man. All I know is both had shiners, and looking at the Councilman now, I could still see some hints of bruising even considering all of this happened months ago.

"Willoughs, if you have a moment, I would like to speak with you outside. Maybe we can take a walk, or take a drive?" the Councilman offered.

I wasn't too sure if I wanted to speak to him anywhere at the moment, but yet a part of me knew I had to. "Uh sure, sir. Jan, do you mind if I take off?"

"Nope, go right ahead. I've got you covered," Jan gave me the thumbs up.

I folded up the box I had been working on, rolled up my sleeve and followed the Councilman out of the store.

The Councilman and I walked around for a while. We walked so long, I almost wondered if I should be concerned. He did land a good one on my old man, after all.

"Peaceful around here this time of year, right?" the Councilman asked, I guess to break the awkwardness.

"Um, yeah. That's why I decided to stay here for the summer," I shrugged.

Indeed, there were only a handful of people lounging around on campus. The grass was a bit greener and the sky was especially clear today. As we continued walking toward the campus pond, I noticed a couple swinging on a large bench under a tree.

This girl laid her head on her guy's lap, with her blonde hair spooling over his lap as he rocked them both back and forth. He caressed her face and she was grinning from ear to ear, allowing the sun to shine brightly on their youth. Ah, to be in love.

I shook my head, although I had a feeling the Councilman briefly saw me looking at the couple. I didn't care, though. I felt numb and just wanted to get this over with, quite honestly.

"Willoughs…" he started. The Councilman paused and fumbled around in his pockets as if looking for something. Then deciding against it, he led us to the nearby bench close to the pond and sat down.

I followed suit and furrowed my brow, scrunched up my face and tilted my head back allowing the sun's rays to engulf me. We sat there for maybe ten minutes before the Councilman took in a deep breath and resumed. "Willoughs, I've done some things in my life that I am not particularly proud of. My God, haven't we all? But there are a great many things I am proud of. My career, my investments, being able to take care of my family. My wife. My children. You don't know how well it does a man to feel he's accomplished what he's supposed to accomplish and more. You don't know." The Councilman hung his head and ruffled his salt and pepper hair. It was then I saw just how tired he really looked.

He paused again for a while. To be honest, I never really know what to say in moments like these. Do you agree? Disagree? Both? Neither? Of course, I don't know what it's like to accomplish anything because I haven't. Well, besides the regular stuff like potty training and graduating high school, but then almost anyone with half a brain could do that. Could I empathize? Well, maybe. I'm sure when I do get somewhere in the next like thirty or so years, I could say this stuff, too. The situation is awkward with older adults and their rhetorics.

"But you know, Willoughs, the one thing I have been proud of probably more than anything? My kids," the Councilman finally declared. "When Alice came into our lives, it was such a bittersweet moment for us. I'm not sure if Alice told you this, but after we had Mason, we found out we couldn't get pregnant anymore and that devastated us. We always dreamed of having a large family and Mrs. Atkins wanted her girl to dress up and do all this girly stuff with." The Councilman chuckled to himself at the memory, and for a moment, I felt included in their family history, their family secret. Alice had mentioned her folks expressing interest in more kids, but I always figured they were too old to try for more.

"Oh wow. No, Alice didn't tell me that much, sir," I murmured, feeling slightly uncomfortable, yet pleased that he would share this with me at the same time.

"Yeah, so you can imagine when Patricia dropped off Alice to us, how we must have felt," the Councilman shrugged and shook his head before he continued. "And it's such a shame and I do regret and apologize for my behavior, first and foremost. That was uncalled for and I feel as though I owe you an apology and an explanation for my behavior, which is why we're here. Please forgive me as well as I'm sure you are wondering when I'm going to get to the point of this, but it is a touchy matter and I really wouldn't even being saying all of this if I didn't like you." The Councilman looked at me earnestly and sincerely. His gray eyes looked extremely weary, yet contrite, and I couldn't help but feel bad for him.

"No sir, I should apologize and have been trying to apologize for some time," I ventured. "It was totally wrong and selfish of me to even think of doing that without really considering why you would keep your daughter away from her mother… and wait, you like me, sir?… but I mean, I didn't mean any harm or foul or anything. I just feel that everyone has a right to know their parents no matter how crummy or awesome they may be and well… I could tell Alice wanted to know her better and I wanted to make it up to her after you know what happened with Lucy and all… and of course you know to add to trying to be a good boyfriend… and - "

The Councilman held up his hands to stop me from going further. You know, I'm really starting to get irritated that people won't let me finish my thoughts.

"Willoughs. I get it. Believe me, I do, and I know where you are coming from and you're not the bad guy at all. I never faulted you or pegged you as one. Yes, your approach may have been misguided, but I know your intentions weren't. You see, when Patricia left Alice for us to take care of, she didn't do much else. No phone calls, no money, maybe a visit or two, if that, but aside from that, nothing. Mind you, Mrs. Atkins and I were better off than most to care for her, which is why she left her with us, but that is no excuse not to see or even inquire about your own child. And Patricia is an intelligent woman. We all went to college together, that's how we know her, and she was so terribly bright. She was well on her way to law school if she hadn't met Alice's father and that's when her life really went downhill." The Councilman stopped and stared at his hands.

Intelligent, bright, dead ringer for Alice? Law school? Met a guy that turned her life into shit? Well, the Councilman did say he liked me and I liked to believe that at least two out of three would work in my favor. I wouldn't want to hold Alice back from anything. I wouldn't even dream of it, not that she would let me if I even ventured to do so anyway.

I started to feel heavy at that moment, though. When I spoke with Patricia, she did make any mention that life hadn't been in her favor, but I was under the assumption that she had at least tried to see Alice or wanted to, but it was the Atkins' who had prevented it. I will admit, I always found them a little uppity myself and wouldn't have blamed her had that been the case.

"So sir, she never contacted you guys about Alice or any-thing?" I braved, hoping there was something redeemable about her.

"No, she hasn't," the Councilman shook his head mat-ter-of-factly. "We're not some cold-hearted family that would have turned her away if she had wanted to see Alice. We would have welcomed it. They have every right to get to know each other at some point. When she left Alice with us, she only asked that we take care of her as best we could. Throughout the years, of course we tried to reach out to her, schedule a visit, something, but there was always a new number or address or occupation." The Councilman sniffed at this last part.

Yet here, I almost questioned his truth. It did take quite some digging up for Rich and I to find her, but we did get a hold of her. Unless maybe now she wanted to be found? But then, why now?

"I guess now she wanted to be found and I almost wonder why," Councilman Atkins reflected my thoughts and gave a half-chuckle. "Almost."

"That's rough, sir. I didn't know it was so…" I struggled to find the right word.

"Complicated?" the Councilman offered and half-grinned under his weary gray eyes.

"Yeah," I half-smiled back. That was an understatement. "Again, I'm really sorry, sir. I meant no harm. But I do have to ask, why are you telling me all of this? I know you said you like me but…?" Again I struggled to find the words. The guy never seemed to like me before. I always felt like he merely tolerated me. I get that feeling from most people, other than Alice and a select few, of course. Or I used to get that from Alice.

"Why?" the Councilman chuckled lightly, showing crow's feet near his gray eyes. "Well Willoughs, you remind me a little of someone very close to me. You have a certain something that I could never quite put my finger on. Despite all the foolish stuff you say or do, somehow I know you never really mean it and you do have a good heart, and I think that probably matters the most. The world already has too many people who don't have one. Plus, you make Alice so happy. I've noticed the difference in her since you two have been together. It's different than before and you got her into truly singing, which has always been something I enjoyed." The Councilman's eyes gleamed at the memory of her on stage. I could tell he was proud of her, and at the same time made me feel proud as well. Maybe I'm not so bad after all, and Alice does have an amazing voice, to put it simply.

"Well sir, to be honest, I never felt as though you cared for me much. Please forgive me for feeling a bit dumbfounded right now," I gathered. "I don't think we've ever even had a full conversation before like this either, I might add."

The Councilman looked towards me with a smirk and said, "I guess we haven't, Willoughs. Trust me when I say I don't like people too easily, but you're okay." The Councilman laughed to himself and I shot him a grin.

We sat there a few moments longer looking out at the pond. The Councilman looked like he wanted to add something else but thought better of it. After a while, he stood up as if to go. "Well Willoughs, it was a good talk. I do have one question for you, though." He put on a more serious face.

"Yes, sir?" I wondered.

"Do you care for Alice, the way that I feel you do?" the Councilman asked, sincerely.

"If you mean do I love her and care about her, yes I do, sir.

Very, very much," I replied sincerely and just as seriously.

"Well Willoughs, I have no real control over what she does. She and I already spoke about my behavior at the concert. I've apologized and stated that I felt you were a good guy. And hey, I know you've been trying to contact her too, so don't think I'm necessarily the one telling her not to reach out to you," he stated.

"Oh..okay?" I almost asked. I figured as much. I mean, I know Alice will do what she wants and if she hadn't gotten back to me at this point, I had a feeling it was more of her own free will than her dad's. Although I was wondering if she would ever call or at least text me back.

"So what I'm saying, Willoughs, is that I'm not holding her back," he restated. "That move and planning that you did for the concert was pretty thoughtful and a huge gesture. If you want to speak with her, my best piece of advice would be to do something on that caliber." He shrugged his shoulders before adding, "Maybe not bringing in Patricia, but that level, if you catch my drift." The Councilman held up his hands as if for emphasis. I had to admit he looked kinda off doing that gesture as it looked a bit young for him to do.

"I catch your drift, sir, but what if that's not even enough?" I wondered aloud seriously.

"Willoughs, if it's meant to happen, it will. All in due time," the Councilman clapped my shoulder. Gosh, I hate it when people get all cliché. It usually means there's nothing left to offer but the obvious, as if that wasn't already obvious.

"Duly noted, sir," I nodded and sighed.

"Hang in there, Willoughs." The Councilman gave me an almost farewell pat on the shoulder. "Take care of yourself." The Councilman walked back through where we came from and off a distance until I couldn't see him anymore past the parking lot.

I glanced back around me and saw that the couple was huddled over the guy's phone looking at some video that made them giggle hysterically. I leaned back into the bench and faced the water once more. I put my hands behind my head and allowed myself to drift off and doze.

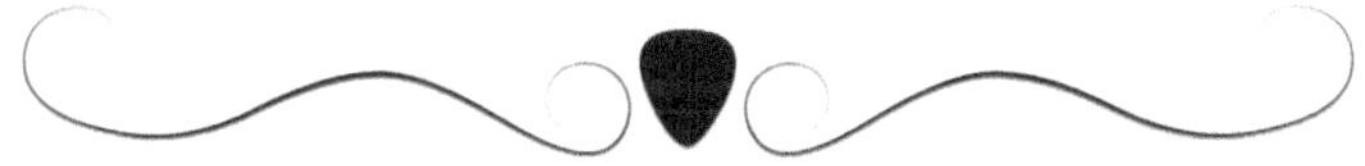

"Will-oohs! Will-oohs! Where are you?" Ella-Bella screamed at the top of her lungs. Man can that girl pierce an eardrum! I sank deeper and deeper under the pile of clothes and junk under my bed. Jeez, even under this mess I could hear her all the way from downstairs!

Her feet treaded lightly on the stair board and I could sense my opponent closing in on me. Hide and seek was always one of our more favorite games to play together, and though I tried to make a promise with myself not to visit for the summer, I couldn't keep it up and had to see Ella-Bella and my folks. So here I was trapped underneath old clothes in the dusty recesses under my bed. I should tell my mom to vacuum more. Ugh.

"Willoughs? Ella-Bella?" our mother called. "Both of you stop playing around! Willoughs, come down so I can talk to you!" Well, speak of the devil.

"Boo! Got ya!" Ella-Bella pounced on the floor just after mom called me down. Her tiny head glanced at me from the other side of the bed and almost caught me off guard.

"Yeah, you got me," I chuckled. I tried to wiggle my way from under my bed to catch her for a tickle fest until my mom called again. "Willoughs, I mean it! Come here now!"

I hurried up to scurry from the cruxes of my bed. "Coming ma!" I yelled over before bending over to scoop Ella-Bella into a mini tickle fest.

"W-w-will-oohs! Stop!" Ella-Bella squealed through tears and giggles.

"No, I must unleash my wrath! Muahaha!" I raspberried into her stomach, which of course only added more to her cries, until I finally plopped her down onto my bed.

"Okay Ella-Bella, let me see what mom wants and I'll be back," I breathed as I wiped at a trail of sweat under my brow.

I made my way downstairs and noticed my mother and father sitting at the dining table, both of their hands clasped against their lips and furrowed brows. My father had long since recovered from the scuffle with Alice's dad, but I did notice he looked almost worn.

I've been noticing that a lot lately, actually. My parents looked more their age every day and a part of that freaked me out. Here were two middle-aged people who were not the bright, youthful parents of the past. I remember thinking the same of our Nana BooBoo, and everyone knows what happens to Nana BooBoo. Though I quickly shook this thought from my mind and focused on my two aging parents in front of me. My dad looked more gray than usual and his crow's feet were definitely more prominent. Yet somehow, I gotta say that despite that, my dad does look pretty rocking. And people do say that despite my red hair, I could totally pass for my dad. So I guess that's something to look forward to.

"What's up? Why do you have the 'we need to talk about deep social matters' face?" I inquired and pulled up a seat at the dining table.

My mom gave a half-smile underneath her hands and looked quickly at my dad, who had been taking long eye reposes. "Well Willoughs-," she began before my dad cut her off.

"Willoughs," my father breathed into his clasped hands. He closed his eyes and exhaled. I felt as though I waited forever until he started to speak again.

"Willoughs, what your father is beginning to say is that we think you should try for Alice again," my mother spoke evenly, finally breaking the silence.

"Margaret!" my father exhaled.

"No," I replied, just as evenly.

My father looked up to me abruptly."Willoughs?"

"It's just as well," I replied even more evenly. "Alice doesn't want me and besides, I think she has some things she needs to figure out for herself before she thinks of being with me again." I felt my shoulders trembling, "And that's not even taking into account what her dad did to you, pops, no offense. I mean, I know you mean well and want me to be happy. Hell - "

"Willoughs!" my mother shrilled. "Language!"

"Right. Sorry," I began again. "Heck, her dad even so much as gave me the green light, but after all I've done to her, I can't add more to what I've already done. Plus, who even knows what I'll screw up in the future? I kissed my ex, I brought back her mother without regard to how her family felt, and even though her dad somewhat likes me now, she's not on the path to becoming a lawyer anymore and that was her dream. I was a distraction and I just don't... I don't deserve her."

There, I said it. Months after all that's happened, and though it hurt like hell, I'd said the ultimate truth. I don't deserve her. I felt hot tears ball up in the back of my eyes and willed myself not to pussy up in front of my folks. It's something I'd known since I laid eyes on her, but the cold, hard truth is that I don't deserve her and never did. All this time, I'd been after someone who was never meant for me. A complete waste of time, if you ask me.

"Willoughs, honey, you can't possibly believe that, do you?" my mother started to sympathize. She sat next to me on my side of the dining table and draped her arm over my shoulder, at first unsure if I would back away or not.

"It's true mom, and it's totally cool. I guess I never wanted to admit it aloud to myself before but it's true," I stated as matter-of-factly as I could.

"Oh Willoughs, Alice is not better than you and if you ask me, you both deserve each other!" my mother proclaimed.

"Son, I've been silent but I have to agree with your mother and that's why we called you down here," my father stated simply.

"Look, with all due respect, I know what you're going to say - " I began before he interrupted.

"Cut the crap, son. Now I don't want you to think your old man's a punk just because I almost lost a squabble on your behalf and want you to go back to that—it's quite the contrary," my father stated. "Did Alice not forgive you when you had that incident with Lucy?"

"Well, she did - " I answered slowly.

"So then she was willing to forgive you and accept that

you did wrong and move past it," he affirmed. "Did Alice not agree to join your band and help you guys out for that competition? Even knowing she would have to multi-task with her own studies and her part-time job amongst other commitments?"

"Well she did, but…" I answered.

"So then she was willing to take on the responsibility of another commitment in addition to being your girlfriend, which I'm sure is another job on its own," my father reasoned, though not without a half-smile on his face. "And did she not go after you that Christmas dinner in the freezing cold, even though she didn't have to?"

"Yeah she did, but…" I replied.

"So then she cared about you enough as a friend and as a person to make sure you were alright," my father again affirmed.

"Yeah but dad, all the stuff you just mentioned was what she sacrificed to be with me. She didn't have to do that, and what good am I to her if she has to always give up something to be with me?" I inquired.

"Son, that's what love is. You give and take. Now from how you've been acting and from how her father has reacted, I'd say she sees something in you worth fighting for," my dad retorted. "Just seeing you two together, I know she's as crazy about you as you are with her, and you want to know what I think?"

"What's that?" I asked, wearily.

"I think that you allow Alice to be more of herself than most people around her," my dad stated firmly.

"What makes you think that?" I wondered.

"Well she often wants to hang around you, and knowing you for eighteen years of your life, that takes dedication and a like mind," my father reasoned. "And a pretty amazing person to realize that and want to be around that."

"Dad, now you're just gassing me up," I shrugged off.

"No Willoughs, everything your dad is saying is true," my mother cut in. "Look at your friends!"

"What about them? We're just regular guys," I pointed out.

"Regular to you maybe, but they're probably some of the most loyal and true friends you could ask for, right?" my mother reasoned.

"I agree, son, and it's not everyday someone can say they have that so you must be pretty special to have them," my father concurred.

"I mean, I guess but…" I wasn't exactly sure how to come back from that.

"And don't think you're inhibiting Alice's dreams either. If anything, you're allowing her to live out her dreams by being in your band," my father further reasoned. "I'm sure if Alice wanted to, she could do anything she put her mind to whenever she wanted to. If you ask me, I think the lawyer thing was partially influenced by her dad, but then again you can have more than one dream and you're giving her more of an outlet to do so."

"Hmm," I rested my head into my hand, and mulled over what my dad said.

"Son, I don't know much about her situation with her biological mother and all, but I'm sure whatever grudge or tension she has against you can be fixed. You had good intentions, which counts, and I'm sure she misses you," my dad said.

"I don't know, dad," I breathed. "I just don't know. She won't even talk to me. I called and texted so many times and to no avail."

"Give her some time, Willoughs, and when the moment is right, then you make the big gesture," my dad half-smiled. He stood up and patted my shoulder.

"When is the right time, though? What's the big gesture? What?" I inquired.

My mother got up to make her way to the kitchen to start preparing dinner and giggled. My dad grinned and stated, "Willoughs, the big gesture is that ultimate gesture you make to show someone that you truly love them. The grand ta-da, if you will. You'll figure it out. When it's the right time, it'll come to you." He chuckled lightly and then made his way up the stairs.

I turned to my mom, who shook her head lightly at what I presume was my own naiveté. "Willoughs, will you help me set the table?"

"Sure thing, mom," I replied.

So many thoughts swirled in my head. Of course my folks were right; they luck out with that often enough. Though getting to this "big gesture" would be tricky given that Alice would never return my calls, much less see me, under the current circumstances. Sure, her father approved, which I could use to navigate that obstacle, but how could I make her hear me out?

"What's got my Willoughs looking so furrowed, hmm?" my mother asked good-naturedly.

As I placed the last plate on the table is when it hit me.

"Mom! I think I know just how to get Alice back!" I exclaimed.

"Are you sure, Willoughs? A minute ago you didn't seem so sure," my mother cautioned.

"No, I think I know just what to do," I replied calmly and confidently. I walked up to her and embraced her warmly. "Thanks so much, mom. I love you." I planted a kiss on her cheek before grabbing one of the apples lying around next to her.

"Okay, if you're sure, Willoughs," my mom expressed, half-concerned. "Alice is a lovely girl, we always liked her. Just be careful whatever you decide. Your father can't afford any more trips to the hospital."

"It'll be fine, mom," I smiled sheepishly before scampering backwards towards the stairs. I needed to call Rich if I wanted to ensure that this was going to go well. I knew what the ultimate "big gesture" I should make was.

"Don't chicken out on this, Willoughs," Mike stated.

"Though are you sure you wanna do this? Here?" Bill questioned.

"We got your back, no matter what, man," Rich clapped my back.

"Whatever, don't mess this up, Willoughs," Chelsea rolled her eyes and giggled. She looked up to Rich and wrapped her arm around his waist. I must say that since she and Rich have finally found common ground a few months ago, she's actually been more tolerable.

"Relax guys, don't make me more nervous than I already am," I sighed. My palms were getting sweaty and I could feel my cheeks burn, yet I knew I had to do this. I peeked out to the quad, and sure enough, there was Alice chatting up with Chester.

I decided to bring the gang out to crash Ubuntu's Back to School Bash to help with my "big gesture." I couldn't stop looking at Alice, though, it had been so long. She looked great as usual as the sun beamed down on her. She was sitting atop a picnic bench, head full of curls tossed back and laughing loudly at something Chester had said. Her teeth were extremely white against her brown skin and her curls looked especially glossy and dark. Her legs, outstretched and glistening beneath her short shorts, almost dangled off the table. She wore a red and green cut Ubuntu shirt that bared her midriff and she looked…content?

She didn't appear sad or too happy, despite laughing at Chester's jokes, so I guess the right word was content. I almost had half a mind to pick up and leave, but at the same time I missed her terribly and wanted to laugh with her and make her happier. My heart practically seized just looking at her. Geez, I need to get a grip and soon.

"Willoughs? Ugh, stop ogling her. You'll get her back soon enough," Chelsea said, half-annoyed, half-sincere. It's funny how I could never get a full well-meaning emotion from her. It always has to be front loaded with another negative connotation.

Deciding to brush off her irritation, I asked her for what might have been the hundredth time, "Are you sure Alice misses me? This isn't going to be a waste, right?"

Chelsea's eyes softened for a moment, as if she could sense my full sincerity. "Willoughs, she misses you. She doesn't say it but I can tell. Besides, I wouldn't agree to this and risk her happiness. I'm not cruel." Chelsea gave a half-smile and for once there were no undertones. Finally, a mostly full positive emotion from this one.

And with that, I felt more assured. "Thanks, Chelsea," I exhaled.

"Yeah yeah, don't get all mushy on me. Save that for Alice," Chelsea shrugged. "Look, let me get back to her before she starts wondering what's taking me so long. You'll be fine." Chelsea started to head back in Alice's direction, and for a brief second looked uncertain, then winked at me before scampering off.

"Ain't she amazing?" Rich gushed. He folded his arms across his chest and gazed at Chelsea as she strutted back towards Alice and Chester.

"Meh, she can have her moments," I relented before turning back to the guys. "Okay, Mike and Bill, you guys remember what we practiced, right?"

"We got you, Willoughs buddy," they both chimed and gave the thumbs up, before backing away to the other side of the pillar.

"Just give us the cue when you're ready, Willoughs," Bill assured, and they walked towards the other side of the quad. Funny, I always find myself faced with these scenarios to step up.

Rich faced me and offered a half-smirk, saying, "You'll do fine, Will. Let's win back your woman!" Rich clapped my shoulders, and before I could lose more of my nerve, left promptly to join the other guys. I inhaled and exhaled. I looked back at Alice continuing her conversation with Chelsea and Chester as if nothing out of the ordinary was going on at all. Almost absentmindedly, and yet almost with re-solve, I gave the boys the cue and fixed my eyes on Alice.

Alice sat a good 100 yards away from the center stage for this event, and if I scampered by without her noticing, all would be cool. The boys had their instruments already onstage and Rich whispered something into the DJ's ear. He nodded his dreadlocked head in affirmation and pulled the mic to his lips as the boys got in place. "All right y'all, this is DJ Ahmed Eazy coming at you! We got a special request from a young gentlemen so give your ears and sweet vibes to our guests!" DJ Ahmed Eazy shut off his spinners and flipped the switch so the guys' audio could be heard. Mike hit his drumsticks together while Bill and Rich strummed their guitars smoothly. I glanced almost hesitantly toward Alice and decidedly ambled onto the stage. I probably shouldn't have glanced at her huge shocked doe eyes, as I found myself tripping going up the stairs and landed flat on my face. Awesome.

I heard a couple snickers from the onlookers and a slight stop in the guitars, and tried my best to peel my face off the step. I could feel a throbbing above my eyes and along my nose, but decided to shake it off and try to regain composure onto the stage. Rich mouthed "Are you okay?" and with a shrug of my wrist, I grabbed the mic, perhaps too aggres-sively, and breathed, "How are you, Ubuntu?!"

A few people gave some claps of encouragement. Alice was staring at me still with wide eyes and her full mouth was slightly open. Chester looked over with bemused inter-est while Chelsea had a faint trace of concern on her face.

I continued. "Now most of you know me probably as that white dude that hangs with Alice or as Willoughs or as gin-ger or whatever. But today I want to perform a little some-thing for you guys on this beautiful afternoon, though this is especially for someone I hold so dear to me. This woman has taught me so much and is someone I honestly want to know forever. Although…" I trailed off a bit as I caught my breath. I looked squarely at Alice, whose initial shocked expression had firmed into a steely concentration on every last word that was coming out of my mouth. "…I hurt her so terribly by doing something that I probably should have left alone. I just want to perform this song for her. And, if we never get back together, I think I'll be okay but I want to do this to show how sorry I really am and that I would never intentionally hurt her. I love you." I met her firm gaze again and noticed her eyes soften for the slightest millisecond before she crossed her arms. I sighed, closed my eyes, and began to sing for Alice.

So, you may think I might not have the best voice around and you would actually be wrong. Well, partly anyway. It's not the best but my voice isn't too shabby, either. Some would even say my voice could compete with Rich's for our lead, but I wouldn't do that to myself. Funnily enough, I have stage fright when it comes to my singing as opposed to my guitar playing but, at least for the time being, I wasn't terribly afraid this time. You might argue it was because my eyes were closed as I only pictured Alice and that she really understood how sorry I was or you might argue that my resolve finally got the best of me. Whatever the case may be, I sang.

There were no interruptions, no technical difficulties, nothing. I just sang. I had written this song for her and played it for the boys the night before, and got a standing ovation. Though that doesn't really matter now. The case in point was that I sang. I willed my tenor register over my mic and let its velvety notes reverberate over the speakers. I admit even I lost myself as I sung and it was no longer as if I was on stage in front of a crowd. I wasn't crooning with my boys backing me up. I wasn't even holding the mic. I just sang my heart out, for Alice.

As I wrapped up my last notes, I slowly opened my eyes. So slow, I hadn't even noticed tears had streamed down my face until I fully opened them.

"...Remember this message for me..." I trailed my last words as the crowd erupted into applause. I blinked my eyes and was immediately taken aback at how many people had gathered around the stage. I glanced over to Alice's direction only to see her try to keep her steel gaze, but I knew those doe eyes were going to tear any moment. As she came to realize this, she turned, got up from the picnic table, and went abruptly in the other direction, walking heavy-footedly away from me. My heart seized a little and I ran off the stage after her.

"You better go get your girl!" I heard a voice yell in the crowd.

"Willoughs! Willoughs!" another voice chanted, until Rich grabbed the mic and started leading them further. I didn't care, though. I ran past Chelsea and Chester.

"Go after her, Willoughs!" I heard Chelsea cheer but I kept after her as Alice, probably noting the cheers, sped up and was actively running away from me.

"Alice! Alice!" I shouted at her, trying to will my voice over the crowd, but she kept running. Her raven curls bounced with each hit her feet took on the ground. Though I was way taller than Alice and should have easily caught up with her by now, I still found myself quite a ways from her. Soon we came up on a path leading to a hill, and when I looked behind me, I noticed the crowd had gotten considerably smaller than it was a few minutes ago. Alice ambled up the hill and soon we came onto a small enclosure at the top that overlooked the rest of the park. Alice suddenly stopped to grasp her knees for breath when we had reached the peak of the enclosure, and then sank onto the ground.

I grasped my knees as well as I had been so intent on catching up with her I hadn't noticed exactly how out of breath I was. I fell down near her on the ground and pulled at my shirt to fan myself. I managed to keep some distance between us as we settled onto the grass.

I looked out back at the path we had just ran to get to this overlook and saw tiny figures quite a ways from us. I could hear Rich and the guys perform faintly and saw what I presumed to be people dancing to our music, and grinned at myself. I turned to look at Alice and noticed she too was looking out at the crowd. We sat there for what seemed like hours in silence. I gathered my nerve to speak when she finally broke the silence in a whisper so small I almost thought I wished her to say it. "Willoughs."

I looked at her. She was looking still at the crowd around the band. She didn't say anything again for what seemed a long time, so that I thought myself insane in thinking she had said something at all.

"Willoughs, I --" she started again before blinking back a couple of tears.

"Alice, please let me speak. I am so so sorry! I love you and I meant everything I've said! I should've spoken to you before I did anything and then I saw your dad that time in the park and I'm an idiot and you have every right to --" words gushed out of my mouth like vomit until a hard slap across my face made me see stars. I clasped the side of my face and stared wide-eyed at her.

"Willoughs, what the fuck!" Alice blazed into my eyes before breaking down into tears and covering her eyes. I rubbed what was probably the reddest face I ever had and then closed the gap between us to embrace her. She sobbed silently and tensely into my shirt at first, before finally giving way to wrap her arms around me. I squeezed her into my arms and relished into this welcome, warm, soft, delicate feeling. I missed this so much and could tell she did too when she finally squeezed me back. I dared myself to kiss the top of her raven curls and was met with strawberry-lavender goodness, one of my most favorite smells. Her.

"I was so upset and angry and relieved and just confused, for so long," she finally muffled into my shirt. She pulled herself away a little from our embrace to look me in the eye. "I forgave you a while ago, Willoughs. Actually, right after my dad told me he had spoken with you in person. I guess this whole time, though, I wasn't so much upset at what you did, but more so at myself and my parents." She wiped away her tears and breathed hard as she rolled her eyes. "All of them." She chuckled softly and I rubbed her shoulder.

"Listen, I was still at fault, though. I shouldn't have pushed for a conversation or a meeting that your family wasn't ready to have, and for that I am truly sorry. Leave it to me to mess with a good thing, right?" I threw a half-smile.

Alice attempted to smile back to me and said, "Yeah but you had the right intentions, Willoughs. It was a conversation that needed to be had and I do thank you for pushing for it, even when we weren't - or I wasn't as ready as I thought I'd be to accept it." Alice laid her head on my shoulder, her sweet strawberry and lavender scent filling my nose again before she started. "I spoke with her, you know. My birth mother." Alice began to twiddle her fingers and I noticed drops of tears falling down onto her hands, slowly, almost mesmerizingly. She swallowed back the lump in her throat and held me tighter. "Thank you, Willoughs. I did need that."

I squeezed her tighter and just held her there. Eventually, we laid back onto the grass, still embraced, and got lost in our thoughts. Yet as we laid there, I knew something had changed, something had shifted between us. Though for some reason, the feeling wasn't good or bad. It just felt like something that had to happen, you know? I found myself kissing the top of her forehead at length, whether it was to comfort her or myself, I wasn't sure, but it was still comforting and as if she belonged there. Like we belonged together.

I sighed as the sun began to set over us and was glad to have her there in my arms watching it with me.

"It's so beautiful," Alice remarked my exact thoughts.

"It is," I agreed.

We continued to gaze at the setting sun, and soon enough, crickets began to chirp to welcome the evening.

"So what happens now?" I finally broke the reverie.

"Hmm?" Alice glanced up, almost sleepily.

"Where do we go from here? Where should we go from here?" I pondered aloud, and almost shocked myself with the second question. Perhaps it was the better question, though, and one that needed to be asked.

Alice rose up steadily from my embrace, making me wish I hadn't asked and that we could lay there forever. She stood up quickly like the pixie she was and dusted herself off. She stretched out her arms and shook her raven curls as if waking from a dream, and I rose to the occasion as well.

"Well I know we should probably get back to the cookout. I know everyone is wondering what's going on, and besides I'm pretty much starving!" Alice giggled.

When she noticed I was actually serious, she returned the

expression and shrugged her shoulders. "...As for where we go from here, Willoughs, who knows? We'll figure it out. That's life, right? Isn't that the point of it all?"

I nodded at this and bit back a smile before turning a devilish grin back up to her. "You know I love you, right, Alice?"

Alice turned on her heel, rolled her eyes playfully, and shook her mass of raven curls. "Yeah yeah, Willoughs. I love ya, too."

I half-ran to catch up with her and placed my arm on her shoulder. "No, no, I really mean it, you know!"

"Sure, Willoughs." Alice threw up a dazzling smile as we walked down the hilled path.

"It's true," I stated, matter-of-factly. "And if I haven't proved it enough already, I'll do you another solid."

"Oh yeah?" Alice raised an eyebrow and added, "and what exactly would that entail?"

"I'm going to tell you my real name!" I proclaimed.

Alice's doe eyes opened up slightly more. "Really, Willoughs? Are you sure? That's kinda huge!" Indeed it was, only my folks and Rich knew my real name. Not even the other guys in the band knew.

"Of course, Alice. I love you and you mean a lot to me, and you should know," I answered sincerely. Her eyes warmed at this and I began again, "Now, a word of caution. When I tell you this, you can't tell anyone else. Not Chelsea, not anyone else. Got it?"

Alice held up three fingers and enthused, "Scout's honor!"

After assessing her for honesty and sincerity, I leaned down to whisper into her ear. "Alright so it's ---"

Alice gasped slightly and clutched her mouth, then caught herself and giggled. "It figures you would have a weird name, W--Willoughs." She busted out laughing and I had to grin along with her. Alice playfully patted my stomach and squeezed me close to her as we made our way back to the gang.

I knew we were going to be fine. Though I wasn't quite sure where we stood together in terms of a formal relationship, I had a feeling whatever awaited us would be for the long haul. As we got closer to the picnic benches where our friends sat and laughed and ate some mean-looking barbecue, I couldn't help but feel that same feeling I had earlier. Something had shifted, with not only Alice and I, but I could feel with the group as well. It was a good feeling, though.

I looked at Rich and Chelsea wrapped up in each other, giggling and just looking happy. Bill was talking to one of the members from Ubuntu, a spirited junior from what I recalled named Amber who was fond of wearing dashikis. Mike and Chester were engaged in some conversation about guitars from the looks of it as Mike frequently pointed and demonstrated to his own guitar.

Taking in all of this and my status with Alice, I knew everything would work itself out. I mean, that is the point after all, isn't it?

END.

Epilogue.

(for those who are interested…)

The Point

So, as you can see, it wasn't totally my fault at all. Yeah, I may have overstepped some boundaries and yeah, I may have gotten myself in some hairy situations. But that really isn't the point. I had the best of intentions as you can see and I fought damn hard to right my wrongs. That's more than what most guys do, even in the most committed relationships. Am I right?

However, that's not the point either and I know you're really tired of me saying that. Hell, I might even retire that word from my vocabulary altogether after this shtick. I guess what I'm really trying to say at the end of the day is this. When you're wrong, fix it. When you're in love, fight for it. And for God's sake, when you get to the point of it all - mean it.

… Also, in case it wasn't clear, my relationship status with Alice is still to be determined, although I'm pretty sure that's going to turn around very, very soon. Exactly five people know my actual name (sorry, you won't get that lucky today!). And I have finally revealed the ultimate point of my telling you all of this. Thank you. Good night.

The Point

Acknowledgements

During my last year of undergrad, I got the inspiration for writing this novel as I was brainstorming an assignment for my creative writing class. I had to tell Willoughs' story! I wrote furiously and had an early draft I felt really good about. However, unlike most of my prior manic moments of inspiration, I wasn't met with writer's block. I knew where I wanted to go with his story.

Fast forward months and a couple short years after that, I finally finished my first novel and this is the story you hold in your hands. I'll be extremely honest—this story wasn't meant to be the next Great American novel. This story was meant to be what it is. A simple, sweet love story. For that, I am extremely proud and hope that you appreciate it for those merits.

I would like to take this space to thank all those who helped me to publish this. Thank you, of course, to my editor, Nadara Merrill for clarifying my work and Willoughs' many run-on thoughts and ramblings! Thank you most definitely to my husband, Wilson Hawkins, for being my main supporter throughout this process and your beautiful cover design. I love you and thank you for your boundless encouragement and sage advice whenever I'm uncertain about anything. Thank you to my friends, family, and colleagues who helped support my artistic and creative expressions. Thank you to the readers, both those who have followed me for a while now and the new. I thank you.

www.ingramcontent.com/pod-product-compliance
Lightning Source LLC
Chambersburg PA
CBHW030745110726
47900CB00008B/2462